FROM THE NANCY DREW FILES

THE CASE: A treasure hunt turns into a desperate search for clues . . . to the identity of a murderer.

CONTACT: The fingerprints on the murder weapon belong to expedition leader Sean Mahoney; the case of proving his innocence belongs to Nancy.

SUSPECTS: Talia Ortiz—Blaming Sean for the diving accident that killed her brother, she may have found the perfect way to exact revenge.

Zach Hardwick—the first mate of Sean's ship, he believes he deserves a larger share of the treasure . . . and may have decided to take it all.

Leif Dorning—Owner of a rival treasure-hunting operation, he may have devised the ultimate business strategy: killing off the competition.

COMPLICATIONS: The true murderer is a master of deceit and disguise. Nancy realizes she must lure the killer into the open . . . using herself as bait.

Books in The Nancy Drew Files® Series

Available from ARCHWAY Paperbacks

The Nancy Drew Files™

Case 85

Sea of Suspicion
Carolyn Keene

AN ARCHWAY PAPERBACK
Published by POCKET BOOKS
New York   London   Toronto   Sydney   Tokyo   Singapore

AN ARCHWAY PAPERBACK *Original*

An Archway Paperback published by
POCKET BOOKS, a division of Simon & Schuster Inc.
1230 Avenue of the Americas, New York, NY 10020

Copyright © 1993 by Simon & Schuster Inc.
Produced by Mega-Books of New York, Inc.

ISBN: 0-671-79477-9

First Archway Paperback printing July 1993

10 9 8 7 6 5 4 3 2 1

NANCY DREW, AN ARCHWAY PAPERBACK and colophon are registered trademarks of Simon & Schuster Inc.

THE NANCY DREW FILES is a trademark of Simon & Schuster Inc.

Cover art by Tricia Zimic

Printed in the U.S.A.

IL 6+

Sea of Suspicion

Chapter

One

MMMM, THIS IS the life," Bess Marvin said dreamily as she tied back her long blond hair with a scarf. "Renting a convertible was a great idea, Nancy."

Nancy Drew smiled and patted the steering wheel of the creamy white sports car she was driving. "I thought a convertible would be fun to have for our drive to Key West," she agreed.

Bess's cousin George Fayne spoke up from the backseat, "It's also the ultimate tanning machine. Right, Bess?"

Bess's blue eyes twinkled as she reached for a bottle of sunscreen in the glove compartment. "You said it. We should have plenty of sun *and* fun on this vacation," she said, rubbing the lotion onto her shoulders. "Think of it—two whole weeks in Key West, Florida."

Nancy smiled at the thought. She, Bess, and George had landed at Miami International Airport early that morning. Now they were nearing the end of the five-hour drive to Key West, the last in a chain of tiny islands that stretched out like piano keys off the southern tip of Florida.

As soon as they reached the island, Nancy slowed down. The ocean drive was dotted with palm trees and old-fashioned, gingerbread houses.

"I love these Victorian homes!" Nancy exclaimed.

With the help of a map they'd gotten from the rental company, the three friends soon found their way to the Sunset Cove Inn, a rambling old hotel that was nestled into a small bay. They checked into their room, which had a ceiling fan and lots of white wicker furniture. Glass-paned French doors opened onto a deck overlooking the sandy beach.

Bess walked out onto the deck. "Smell the ocean," she said, closing her eyes and inhaling deeply. "I could spend the whole two weeks right here on this beach."

"Forget it, Bess," George called from inside the room. "I've got the rest of the day planned for us." George held up a guidebook as she and Nancy joined Bess on the deck.

"That's right," Nancy said. "We have a reservation on an island tour boat. In fact, we'll have to hurry if we want to make it to the marina by two o'clock."

Bess groaned and flopped onto a lounge chair. "Have you two forgotten that vacations are for relaxing?" she asked.

"Come on, Bess," Nancy coaxed. "A little sight-seeing never hurt anyone."

"Besides, this should be really exciting." George had opened the guidebook and was reading from it. "We're going on board a treasure-hunting boat called the *Lady Jane*. The owners give private tours to raise money for their expeditions."

"Real treasure? Like gold and diamonds and stuff?" Bess suddenly sounded more interested.

George nodded. "According to this book, there are at least two thousand sunken ships off the coast of Key West," she said, brushing back her curly, dark bangs. "And lots of them, they think, are old Spanish galleons that went down with treasure on board."

"Just think of all that gold and silver under the sea," Bess mused. "Now *there's* a mystery for you, Nan."

"No, thanks!" Nancy protested, and laughed. "This trip is strictly R and R."

At eighteen Nancy's sleuthing skills had already brought her fame as a detective. She had just finished solving an important case back in her hometown of River Heights. Now she was looking forward to taking a break from crime.

Nancy and her friends changed into shorts and T-shirts, stuffed jackets and extra gear into a bag and set off for the King Point Marina. Nancy drove very slowly to avoid a mishap with the many bicyclists. It seemed as if everyone preferred walking or bicycling to driving on the small island. In less than five minutes they were pulling into the parking lot of the marina, which lay just a mile down the shore from their hotel.

The marina was crowded with boats of all shapes and sizes, and in the harbor beyond, sails dotted the horizon.

"There's our boat, right over there," George said. She pointed to a large vessel that was tied at a nearby slip. Its white hull was long—George estimated its length to be about fifty feet. The deck was covered with high-tech equipment.

Nancy could see a tall man and an ebony-haired woman working forward on the bow. The boat's name, *Lady Jane,* was written across the stern in blue letters.

"Ahoy!" George called out to a deeply tanned, muscular young man who was cleaning some scuba gear closer to them on the rear deck.

The young man raised his head at the sound of George's greeting. He was about twenty-five years old, and was wearing cut-off jeans and a light blue shirt. His face brightened when he spotted George.

"Hi there!" He smiled warmly at the girls. His hair had been bleached to light brown by the sun, and his eyes were green.

"I'm looking for Sean Mahoney," George said.

"That's me," he replied, straightening up and stepping smoothly off the boat onto the dock. "Owner and skipper of the *Lady Jane*. What can I do for you?"

"I'm George Fayne," George replied. "We spoke last week about your island tour."

George introduced Sean to Nancy and Bess. While they were talking, Nancy noticed that Sean kept glancing at George.

"Let's go on board. I'll introduce you to the crew," Sean said, touching George's arm lightly. "I was thinking of calling off today's tour because a party of ten just canceled on me. It's expensive to take the boat out for only a couple of people, but I guess I can make an exception in your case."

As Sean and George led the way, Bess nudged Nancy's elbow. "I can't believe it. We just got here, and George has already dazzled a cute guy," she whispered, grinning.

Nancy nodded. George and Sean really were hitting it off. She overheard them talking with mutual enthusiasm about scuba diving. As Nancy watched them together, she felt a slight tug at her heart.

Bess spoke knowingly, "You're missing Ned, right?"

"I am," Nancy admitted with a sigh. Just a week earlier Ned Nickerson, her longtime boyfriend, had had to cancel his plans to go on this vacation because of a last-minute crisis at his summer job. "I know he needed to take care of things at the insurance company, but I can't help being disappointed," she confided to Bess.

Bess gave her friend a quick hug. "Well, let's try to have a great time, anyway," she said soothingly.

"G'day, landlubbers!" Nancy turned to see an older man with a weather-beaten face smiling at them from a doorway that led below to the cabins. "I'm Rusty Jones, ship's cook and bottle washer," he announced with a toothy grin. "I hope you girls like conch chowder and Key lime pie, 'cause that's what we're having to eat today," he said.

Rusty stepped forward to join the rest of the group on the deck, which was crowded with all sorts of diving gear and supply bags. As he approached, Nancy noticed that he walked with a slight limp.

"Rusty's what we call an 'old salt,'" Sean said, glancing at the cook. "He grew up sailing and boating around here. He used to be my best diver."

"I'd *still* be the best—if you'd let me prove it," Rusty replied with a trace of bitterness. He reached past Sean and picked up a supply bag that was overflowing with cooking supplies.

"Rusty, we've been through this before," Sean said quietly.

"Sean thinks I can't dive with this bum knee," Rusty explained to the girls, hoisting the bag over his shoulder. "But a fish swims without knees, and so can I." Rusty turned away silently and disappeared back down the companionway leading to the galley.

Sean seemed to be embarrassed by the cook's remarks. "I know Rusty thinks I'm unfair not to let him dive, but he has bad arthritis," he said uncomfortably. "He just can't dive safely anymore."

Nancy spotted a tall, rangy man making his way back to them from the bow. She recognized him as the man she'd seen working up there a couple of minutes earlier. He had pulled a cap on over his close-cropped hair now.

"This is my first mate, Zach Hardwick," Sean said when the man reached them. Zach had pale gray eyes that seemed bleached of all color by years in the sun.

Zach nodded to the girls, then said to Sean, "I'll get the engine started." He added something else in a whisper, but Nancy could make it out: "I hope we don't have any trouble today." Sean only answered him with a glare. Zach shrugged and turned to stride back to the pilothouse, a small enclosure near the bow that housed the ship's steering wheel.

Nancy couldn't help wondering what kind of trouble the first mate meant.

"I'll take you girls forward so Talia, our marine archaeologist, can tell you about the tour and how we run the ship," Sean explained hurriedly.

They walked along a narrow side deck to the bow.

Nancy spotted the slender young woman she'd seen when they first arrived at the ship. The woman walked the short distance to greet the girls.

"I'm Talia Ortiz—pleased to meet you," she said, smiling pleasantly. Talia's gleaming black hair was pulled back into a single braid. She had high cheekbones and large, hazel eyes.

"This is Nancy, George, and Bess," Sean told Talia. "Give them the lowdown on the boat, would you, Talia? I'm going to help Zach get under way." With that, he headed for the pilothouse.

The *Lady Jane*'s powerful engine roared to life, and soon the ship was slicing through the blue-green waters beyond the harbor.

Talia looked at the girls. "For our tour today

we'll be circling the island and stopping at places where we're likely to see local wildlife," she explained. "Yesterday we were lucky and saw a family of dolphins."

"Why is Sean's ship called the *Lady Jane?*" Bess asked.

"*Lady Jane* is the name of the first sunken treasure ship Sean ever found, *La Señora Juana.* Sean just Anglicized it," Talia explained.

"What kind of treasure is Sean looking for now?" Nancy wanted to know.

"We've spent the past year looking for the wreck of the *Ninfa Marina,* a Spanish galleon," Talia explained. "She was the flagship of a Spanish fleet that went down in a storm off Key West in 1653."

"*Ninfa Marina*—that means 'mermaid' in English, doesn't it?" Nancy said.

Talia nodded. "Only *this* mermaid was a treasure ship carrying a load of gold bars and jewels that would be worth about fifty million dollars today."

"Wow!" Bess gasped.

Talia showed them around, reeling off the names of some of the high-tech gadgets used in treasure hunting, like the proton magnetometer and sidescan sonar. She said that both of these enabled the crew to comb the ocean floor for signs of old wrecks.

Nancy stared at a small, tubular craft tethered

to the side of the *Lady Jane.* "That almost looks like a tiny submarine," Nancy said to Talia. "Do you use it in your underwater searches?"

The archaeologist nodded. "That's *Rover,* our manned submersible unit," she explained.

Nancy caught sight of Zach in the pilothouse and remembered what she'd overheard him say to Sean. "Has there been trouble on board recently?" Nancy asked. "Zach mentioned something about it."

Talia paused before answering. "I guess he was talking about the little mishaps that have occurred," she said. "But they're nothing to worry about," she added quickly.

"Then nothing serious has happened?" George asked.

"Not this year," Talia replied, a shadow crossing her face as she turned away.

"What is it, Talia?" Nancy prodded.

Talia faced the girls again. "It's just that talking about this reminds me of my brother, Jaime. He was killed last year in a diving accident," she said, her voice breaking slightly. "He was working for Sean at the time."

Nancy reached out to touch the young woman's shoulder. "I'm so sorry if our questions brought back painful memories," she said gently.

Talia shook her head. "I'm okay."

Just then Nancy felt the boat slow down.

Talia frowned. "That's funny," she said.

"We're not at our first tour stop yet." Her frown changed to an expression of puzzlement as she drew in a deep breath. "That smells like smoke."

Nancy sniffed the air. Talia was right— something was definitely burning. Nancy peered toward the stern where a layer of heavy smoke was rising from the aft deck.

"Look at that smoke!" she cried. "The *Lady Jane* is on fire!"

Chapter

Two

Nancy raced toward the *Lady Jane*'s stern, with Talia and the others on her heels. She arrived on the rear deck just in time to see Rusty running, clutching a red fire extinguisher.

"Fire in the hold!" he yelled. "I think it's in the engine hatch!" A stream of oily-smelling gray smoke was seeping up around the edges of the floor panels on the rear deck. The fire had to be underneath those panels, Nancy realized.

Zach grabbed Rusty's arm to prevent him from opening the floor panels.

"Don't open the hatch—the oxygen will just feed the fire!" Zach shouted. "I'll go turn on the foaming system." He hurried forward to the pilothouse. After a few moments Nancy heard a loud whooshing from underneath the floor panels.

"Thank goodness, it sounds like Zach got the foaming system working," Talia said. "It releases a layer of foam inside the engine to put out any kind of fire."

As if to confirm Talia's words, the smoke began to dissipate.

Sean dashed up onto the deck from inside the ship. "I was in my cabin," he said breathlessly. His face blanched as he surveyed the scene and took in the situation. "Stand back, everyone," he ordered.

Gingerly he removed the engine hatch. Below deck the engine was covered with a layer of foam mixed with black ashes. Sean stared glumly at the mess. "It's not safe to try to fix this at sea," he announced. "We'll have to call the Coast Guard for a tow." He half-smiled at Nancy, George, and Bess. "I'm afraid this ruins your tour."

"Don't worry about that," Nancy said, reassuring him. "What do you think happened?"

Sean shook his head, bewildered. "We have a very sensitive fire detector that's supposed to sound an alarm at the very first hint of smoke," he said. "Why do you think the alarm didn't go off?" he asked Zach, who had returned from the pilothouse.

"I'll check it out, Sean," the first mate replied. "There've been too many weird things going on around here lately," Zach mumbled, turning to

13

go. "I'll radio the Coast Guard," he called over his shoulder.

Nancy heard a sound and watched as Rusty collapsed onto a deck chair. His face was ashen. "Did you see anything when the fire started, Rusty?" she asked him.

"I don't want to talk about it," he snapped. "I just smelled smoke and ran up with the fire extinguisher—isn't that enough?"

Nancy was struck by the cook's defensiveness.

Sean, too, acted mystified by Rusty's response. "Maybe you'd better go lie down for a while, Rusty," he finally suggested.

The cook shook his head. "I'm okay," he insisted. "If any of you want to come with me to the galley, I'll fix you up with a slice of Key lime pie," he offered.

"I could go for some pie," Bess told him. "But just a sliver."

"I'll take one, too," Talia added quickly, and followed Bess and Rusty through the doorway that led down to the ship's galley.

Nancy and George sat hunched over the edge of the engine hold, watching as Sean scooped foam up from the engine into a plastic bucket.

"Is this the kind of trouble that Zach was talking about earlier?" Nancy asked pointedly.

Sean heaved a sigh. "We've had several unexplained incidents like this recently," he reluctantly admitted. "Normally I wouldn't even mention them. Wouldn't want to scare off the paying customers."

"Don't worry about scaring Nancy," George said. "She's a detective."

"A detective? Really?" Sean asked. Then he sighed. "It would take a sleuth to figure out what's been going on around here, that's for sure."

You're on vacation, Drew, Nancy reminded herself. Still, she couldn't resist saying, "Tell me everything that's happened—from the beginning."

"It all started about six months ago," Sean began. "That was when I found a gold ingot belonging to the *Ninfa Marina*."

"Talia told us about the ship—it was a Spanish treasure galleon, right?" Nancy said.

Sean nodded. "Ever since I found that ingot things have been going haywire. We've had a mysterious fuel leak, damaged equipment, and now this fire."

"How awful!" George exclaimed sympathetically.

"At first I thought they were all just accidents," Sean explained. "But now I'm beginning to suspect sabotage." He frowned, scooping more foam into the pail. "To make matters worse, we've had

15

some run-ins with another treasure hunter. His name is Leif Dorning. He runs a big outfit called Sea Scavengers."

"What kind of run-ins?" Nancy asked.

"He deliberately ran his boat over our equipment towline last week and cut it," Sean said indignantly. "We had to send a diver down to retrieve the monitoring equipment we'd been towing."

"Do you think that Dorning might be the one who's been sabotaging your ship?" Nancy asked.

Sean nodded his head. "He'd probably do anything to find the treasure of the *Ninfa Marina,* but I don't have any proof that these mishaps *are* sabotage or that Dorning's responsible."

Sean focused intently on something he had scooped up with the foam. "What's this?" he murmured. He brushed the foam away from the remains of a folded rag.

Nancy crinkled up her nose, then reached out and lifted the rag to sniff it. "This has been soaked in gasoline," she stated.

"Gasoline!" Sean exclaimed. "I guess that answers our question about sabotage," he said grimly.

Nancy nodded. "I don't think there's any doubt that this fire was deliberately set," she agreed. "The question is—by whom?"

"Your friend Dorning?" George volunteered.

Sean thought for a moment. "One of his men could have tossed the rag into the hold before we set sail and let the engine's heat ignite it."

Nancy hesitated before adding, "Or maybe one of your crew set the fire. Maybe someone who's working for Leif Dorning."

Sean shook his head. "I refuse to think that one of my crew could be involved," he said adamantly.

"You have to consider all the possibilities," Nancy said gently.

Sean's shoulders slumped forward. "This situation has gotten totally out of hand," he said, wearily rubbing his eyes. "I can't afford any more problems with this expedition. Last year we lost a member of our crew in a diving accident."

"Talia told us about her brother Jaime being killed," Nancy said.

Sean sighed. "We all took it pretty hard." He stared out to sea, then slowly swiveled and leveled his gaze at Nancy. "I hate to ask you this—I mean, we've only just met—but I'd be grateful if you could help me figure out what's going on."

"Well, we're supposed to be on vacation," Nancy said hesitantly. "But I guess we could do a little sleuthing, too," she added.

"All right!" George exclaimed, flashing Nancy a grateful smile.

* * *

A short time later Nancy, George, and Bess were standing in Sean's cabin under the ship's bow.

"This is where I keep the gold ingot from the *Ninfa Marina,*" Sean said. He opened a cabinet next to his bunk. "We found it all by itself near the end of a reef. It must have drifted from the wreck site because we didn't find anything else in the immediate area."

Inside the cabinet was a metal safe. Sean twirled the dial until they heard a click. Then he opened the door and pulled out a shiny gold bar.

Bess was obviously impressed. "How much is a gold bar like that worth?" she asked.

"About ten thousand dollars on today's market," Sean replied.

Nancy turned the gold bar over in her hand. "Were you planning to sell it?" she asked.

Sean shook his head. "It's more valuable to me as a fund-raising tool. When investors see this hunk of gold, they're much more likely to invest in my company, Atlantic Deep Ocean Technology," he explained.

"How many investors do you have?" Nancy said.

"Eight major ones," Sean replied. "So far I've raised enough money to be able to hunt for treasure for another six months or so."

Nancy handed the ingot back to Sean. "Who else knows about this ingot?" she asked.

"Everyone on my crew—and just about everyone in Key West, too," Sean said. "I'm afraid we treasure hunters have a tendency to brag when we stumble across a find," he added sheepishly.

"Maybe the person who set the fire wanted to steal the gold bar," George suggested.

Nancy shook her head. "It's more likely that they'd want to stop Sean from finding the rest of the treasure," she said.

"What do you plan to do first?" Bess asked a few minutes later when the girls were back on deck.

Nancy pressed her lips together thoughtfully. "I want to question the crew—especially Rusty," she said. "I got the impression he wasn't telling everything he knew about the engine fire."

Nancy left George and Bess leaning on the rail, staring out to sea, and headed for the galley. She found the cook stirring a pot on the stove. When he saw her he smiled and asked, "Want some pie?"

"No, thanks," Nancy replied. "Actually I wanted to ask you some more questions about the fire today."

Rusty glanced shrewdly at Nancy. "Why are you so interested in that fire?" he asked.

"Just curious," Nancy said simply. "Did you notice anyone near the engine before the fire broke out?" she asked.

19

Rusty plopped a lid onto the pot he'd been stirring. "No, I didn't. I wasn't even on deck at the time. Like I said, I smelled smoke, ran up and saw it, then I went for the extinguisher," he said flatly. "You seem like a nice young lady, Miss Drew—so let me give you a piece of advice. Don't go sticking your neck out for Sean. It isn't worth it. Look at me," he complained. "I worked hard for him for three years, and what reward did I get? A cook's job in a stuffy galley."

The shrill blast of a ship's horn cut through the air. "I hope that's the Coast Guard," Rusty muttered.

Nancy ran up on deck. Everyone was clustered together on the stern, watching a black-hulled boat approach.

Sean was glaring. "That's Dorning's *Sea Scorpion*," he said to Nancy. "It figures that he'd show up when we're stuck like this."

Nancy could see a tall, broad-shouldered man with wavy blond hair at the helm of the *Sea Scorpion*. He had to be Leif Dorning, she realized. A couple of burly crew members were standing on the bow.

Dorning threw back his head and laughed heartily. "Bad luck, Sean," he called out with mock sympathy. "I'm afraid I don't have time to give you a tow. I'm hot on the trail of the *Ninfa Marina*."

"You're lucky I didn't report that incident with

the equipment line last week, Dorning," Sean yelled. "You'd better keep your distance from now on."

"At the rate you're going, I won't need to keep my distance," Dorning taunted. "Anyway, you can consider last week a payback. See you later." With a wave, Dorning pushed the *Scorpion*'s throttle forward and roared off.

Sean shook his head. "Dorning's what we call a blow-and-go treasure hunter," he said to Nancy. "He and his crew destroy the natural seabed environment at the sites they excavate."

"He sounds like a real jerk," George fumed.

"What did Dorning mean by 'payback'?" Nancy asked.

"Beats me," Sean said, shrugging.

On the horizon Nancy spotted another ship approaching at high speed.

Zach peered at the boat through a pair of binoculars. "That's the Coast Guard," he said, dropping the glasses. "I'll go signal them."

"Wait, Zach," Sean said. He faced the tall man and Talia. "I want you to know that Nancy's going to help me investigate everything that's been going on here," he told them.

Nancy bit her lip and hoped her frustration didn't show. She hadn't wanted Sean to make her investigation general knowledge. She'd have to tell him not to blow her cover to anyone else.

Talia seemed surprised by Sean's announcement. "I'm a detective," Nancy explained, trying to sound casual. "I just need to ask all of you a few questions."

Zach wheeled around to face Nancy just then —his long, thin face strangely agitated. "Sean's afraid to tell you the real reason for our bad luck," Zach said, his pale gray eyes blazing. "He won't tell you why Talia's brother was killed."

Nancy stared at the first mate, open-mouthed.

"Tell her, Sean. Tell Nancy about the curse of the *Ninfa Marina!*"

Chapter

Three

Cut it out, Zach!" Talia cried, the yellow flecks in her hazel eyes glittering gold. "I won't listen to you blame my brother's death on some old sailor superstition."

"Calm down, you two," Sean intervened. "Zach, I think you owe Talia an apology."

Zach bristled for a moment. Then he blinked. "Sorry if I upset you, Talia," he mumbled at last.

"No harm done—I guess," Talia said. She headed down the side deck toward the bow. "Come on, Sean," she said, "Let's get the lines ready for the Coast Guard."

As soon as Sean and Talia disappeared, Zach spoke. "I didn't mean to upset Talia by mentioning the curse," Zach said. "She's a scientist, so she can't allow herself to believe in that kind of thing."

23

Bess's blue eyes widened. "What kind of curse are you talking about?"

"A lot of folks around here say that anyone who searches for the wreck of the *Ninfa Marina* is doomed to die a horrible death," Zach said quietly.

"Do you believe the *Ninfa Marina* is cursed, Zach?" Nancy couldn't keep the skepticism out of her voice.

"Ever since we found that gold ingot, things have been happening to us—bad things," he said grimly. "Maybe there *is* a curse."

"But Talia's brother was killed *before* you found the ingot," Nancy pointed out.

"That's true, but Jaime was killed on the very first dive we made to find that ship," Zach replied.

"How was he killed?" George asked.

Zach's face darkened. "I was alone on the *Lady Jane* that day. The rest of the crew had gone down to check out a formation. Jaime never came back up." Zach studied his feet. "Bad oxygen mix, the autopsy said. But the stuff in the other divers' tanks seemed all right."

"So Jaime's death was the first of the strange incidents you blame on the curse," Nancy said thoughtfully.

"That's right," Zach said.

"By the way, Zach—where were you when the flames broke out today?" Nancy asked.

The mate's face registered surprise at Nancy's question. "I was in the pilothouse," he explained. "When I heard Rusty shouting about a fire, I ran out and joined him."

Their conversation was interrupted as the coast guard cutter pulled alongside the *Lady Jane.* Zach went foward to help Sean and Talia attach a towline from the other vessel.

During the long ride back to port, Nancy, George, and Bess sat on deck chairs and watched the crew check out the engine. Sean seemed very subdued as he worked silently beside Zach and Talia.

"I think that fire really hit him hard," George observed. Bess leaned over and whispered something in George's ear. "That's a good idea," Nancy heard George say. Then George rose from her chair and walked toward the hatch that led down into the ship.

"Where's George going?" Nancy asked Bess.

"You'll see," Bess said with a grin.

While George was gone, Zach and Talia went forward to gather more equipment.

When George reappeared on deck, she was holding a plate with a slice of pie on it. "Here, Sean," she said, and held out the plate to him. "Bess was sure that a piece of pie would lift your spirits."

"Thanks, George—thanks to all of you guys." Sean smiled at Nancy and Bess. He wiped his hands off with a rag and took the pie. "Meeting *you* has lifted my spirits," he said softly to George. "Would you like to go swimming tomorrow?" he asked. "I know a great little beach."

Nancy thought she spied a slight blush creep up George's face. "Sure," her friend replied.

"Okay, you two." Nancy rose from her chair and walked toward them. "Back to business. Sean, what did Zach find out when he checked the fire alarm? Why didn't it go off?"

Sean shook his head. "We can't figure it out," he said. "There doesn't seem to be anything wrong with it. Just another mysterious malfunction. I'm almost beginning to believe in the curse," he joked weakly.

"Why does Zach believe the wreck is cursed?" Nancy asked.

"Folks around the Keys love to swap stories about sunken ships, especially treasure galleons," Sean explained. "I'm sure someone said the *Ninfa Marina* was cursed as a joke and someone else took it seriously. That's how these legends and superstitions get started."

"Well, at least we know that the engine fire wasn't caused by any curse," Nancy said, lowering her voice. "Sean, I think we should keep my role in the investigation under wraps for the moment."

Sean thumped his forehead with the heel of his

palm. "And I just blew it by telling the crew, didn't I?"

Nancy shrugged. "It's okay. Let's just concentrate on my keeping a low profile from now on."

"I still can't believe that any of my crew would be involved in this," Sean said sadly.

"It's possible that no one on your ship is involved," Nancy replied. "I just have to rule out the possibility before we look other places for suspects."

As soon as they arrived back at the marina, Sean and Zach started the actual work on the *Lady Jane*'s engine. "We're going to need a new pressure gauge," Sean said. "I'll head over to Hank's and pick one up." Nancy saw him glance at George.

"Would you like some company?" George asked with a smile.

"I was hoping you'd offer." Sean grinned, including Nancy and Bess in the warmth of his smile. "Why don't you tag along, too? I can show you around the marina."

"Sure thing," Nancy agreed.

Hank's Place was an old clapboard diving and engine shop at the edge of the marina. The shop had seen better days. Pieces of equipment, new and old, were piled everywhere.

A stocky, red-haired man was tinkering with an engine in the front yard of the shop.

"Hey, Hank," Sean called out. "Nancy, George, and Bess—this is Hank Morley. He owns this place."

"Having more engine trouble, are you?" Hank asked, rising and dusting off the knees of his well-worn overalls. "You know where everything is, Sean. Help yourself."

As Sean nodded and went inside the shop, Hank stared after him. "Seems like Sean's in here every other day finding something to help fix the *Lady Jane,*" Hank said. "I guess that's the price of treasure fever."

"Treasure fever?" Bess repeated. "What do you mean?"

Hank wiped some engine grease off his hands onto a filthy rag. "That's what treasure hunters get when they're after a mother lode like the *Ninfa Marina,*" he said. "It eats away at them. They spend every moment thinking about their ship—and the treasure."

"You sound like someone who knows," George commented, smiling.

Hank nodded. "I used to be a treasure hunter and managed to find just enough gold to buy this shop. Now I only dabble on the weekends. No more treasure fever for me."

Sean came out of the shop with the new gauge. "Put it on my tab, Hank," he called to the shopkeeper.

The sun was beginning to hang low on the horizon. "Has anyone thought about dinner?" Bess asked. "I'm famished."

"It *is* getting late," Nancy replied. "We should probably head back to the inn."

"I'll come by and pick you up tomorrow morning," Sean said to George.

After he left, Nancy, Bess, and George made their way back to their car.

George's face glowed in the red light of the sunset. "I can't believe it, guys," she confided to Nancy and Bess. "I know I just met Sean, but I really *like* him. Is it possible to go for a guy after only one day?"

"Sure—it happens to me all the time." Bess grinned.

"I can see why you like him, George," Nancy said. "He's very cute."

"And charming—in an older-guy kind of way," Bess chimed in.

George tied a sweater around her shoulders before climbing into the convertible. "Flirting's not usually my style, but it can be fun!" she said as they drove off.

Early the next morning Sean knocked on the door of the girls' room.

"Hi, Nancy," he said when she opened the door. "Is George ready to go?"

"You bet!" George said from where she was standing behind Nancy.

"I was going to have Rusty pack us some pastries for breakfast at the beach, but I couldn't find him anywhere," Sean said to George. "We'll have to grab something on the way."

"We'll meet you back at the ship after your swim," Nancy said to Sean. "Say about noon?"

"Great!" he replied. "We can ask Rusty to whip up some sandwiches for lunch."

After Sean and George left, Nancy and Bess headed downstairs for breakfast. As they passed through the inn's lobby, Bess was drawn to a brightly colored brochure that advertised a treasure ship museum.

"Look, Nancy!" Bess cried, holding up the glossy pamphlet. "This says they've got heaps of emeralds on display at the museum. Emeralds are my absolute favorites!"

Nancy grinned at Bess's enthusiasm. "I wouldn't mind seeing the museum myself," she said, flipping through the brochure. "Maybe we'll pick up some information about treasure hunting that will help on the case."

"Look at those diamonds!" Bess squealed, pointing to a sparkling tiara in the museum. "Imagine being the queen who wore these jewels," she said dreamily.

As Nancy stepped forward to improve her view, she was rudely jostled by someone.

"Hey!" she exclaimed, and turned to see a man with a brown beard disappear into the crowd.

"What happened?" Bess asked.

"Oh, nothing," Nancy replied. "Someone just bumped into me and didn't even apologize."

"Some people can be so rude," Bess said.

"Let's forget it," Nancy said, examining another display case. "Get this—the ship's treasure is worth more than four hundred million dollars," she said, reading from a plaque.

"That kind of money is enough to give *anyone* treasure fever," Bess commented.

Bess was right, Nancy realized. Their quick tour had given Nancy a better understanding of the prize that motivated treasure hunters like Sean and his rival, Leif Dorning.

Nancy and Bess left the museum to head back to the King Point Marina to investigate a little before Sean and George got back.

As she was driving, Nancy checked the rearview mirror several times.

"What do you keep looking at, Nancy?" Bess asked curiously.

Nancy squinted to get a better look in the mirror. "I'm *sure* I saw the man driving the car behind us at the museum," she said. "He was the one who bumped into me."

31

Bess craned her neck to peer over her shoulder. "No wonder you remember him," she said. "He's creepy looking."

"He's followed us the whole way," Nancy said.

"Why would he do that?" Bess asked.

"I'm not sure," Nancy replied, "but I'm going to try something. Hang on, Bess."

After checking to make sure there were no pedestrians or bicyclists, Nancy made a sudden right turn into a small alley. She heard the brakes of the car behind them squeal as the bearded man obviously tried unsuccessfully to follow them. Nancy cautiously maneuvered the convertible through a maze of small streets until she was sure she had lost the bearded man.

Bess's knuckles were white from clutching the dashboard. "Wow!" she said. "I guess he *was* following us. Do you think we lost him?" she asked.

"I think we gave him the slip," Nancy replied. "I wonder who he is." She frowned. "Maybe Sean knows."

Nancy and Bess were surprised to spot George and Sean on the dock next to the *Lady Jane*. The couple appeared to be having an intense discussion.

"Looks like things are heating up romantically between George and Sean," Bess observed.

"I don't know," Nancy said, puzzled. "I wonder why they're back early."

Sean raised his head as Nancy and Bess approached. "I've had some bad news," he said. "Rusty Jones has disappeared—and so has my gold ingot!"

Chapter

Four

Y OUR GOLD INGOT has been stolen!" Nancy gasped. "How? When?"

"I guess someone broke into the ship last night and jimmied open the safe," Sean said angrily. "George and I found out about it when we stopped by here on the way to the beach."

"You said Rusty is missing—so you think he stole the ingot," Nancy said.

Sean nodded vehemently. "When George and I arrived this morning, I found out that Rusty hadn't shown up today. Zach and I went by his house to look for him. The door wasn't locked, so we went in and discovered that Rusty's clothes and suitcases were missing."

"Then it is possible Rusty took the ingot," Nancy said.

"You bet it's possible!" Sean exclaimed. "He

must have been behind the sabotage of the *Lady Jane,* too, because I wouldn't let him dive anymore."

"I think we need more facts before we can draw any conclusion," Nancy cautioned. Still, she had to admit that Sean's theory made sense. "Have you called the police?" she asked.

"Not yet," Sean said. "I've been too busy trying to chase Rusty down. Zach's out looking for him, too."

"Let's give the police something to go on," Nancy said. "If we search Rusty's apartment, maybe we'll turn up a lead."

Rusty's home was a second-floor apartment just a few blocks from the marina.

Nancy quickly surveyed the small dwelling. Every bookcase and shelf was jammed with ocean trinkets and nautical memorabilia. An elaborate model ship that must have taken years to construct took up one whole shelf.

"It seems odd that Rusty would have left so many personal things behind," she said thoughtfully.

"Maybe he left in a hurry," George suggested.

Wrinkling her nose, Bess said, "One thing's for sure—he was really sloppy. I've never seen such a mess!" She gestured toward the books and papers that were strewn across the floor.

Nancy knelt down and first began leafing

through the papers, then she picked up one of the larger books. It was oddly weighted. She lifted the cover and gasped at what she found.

"Sean, look at this!" Nancy called excitedly. The pages of the book had been hollowed out and hidden inside was the missing gold ingot!

The four of them stared at the ingot, amazed. "I can't believe you found it just like that," Bess said.

Sean reached for the gold bar. "Well, that cinches it," he said. "Rusty stole the ingot and hid it here."

"Why wouldn't he take it with him?" Nancy asked slowly. "It seems kind of risky to leave it in an unlocked apartment." She stared at the bar in Sean's hands. "Now that we've found it, we have to call the police."

"I'm not going to stay around here and wait for the police," Sean said heatedly. "I know all of Rusty's hangouts. It's only a matter of time before I find him."

Nancy was worried that Sean might do something rash. "Be careful, Sean," she warned. "Remember, you don't know the whole story yet."

"I know all I need to know." Sean was fuming. "I'm going to track Rusty down right now, no matter what." He moved toward the door.

"Wait a minute, Sean," Nancy said. When he paused, she continued, "Let's meet at the *Lady Jane* later this afternoon. We can compare notes then on what we've found. I'll put off calling the police until then."

"Fine," Sean said. "I'll see you at three." He strode out of the apartment, Rusty's screen door banging behind him as he left.

"I hope Sean doesn't do anything dumb," Nancy said, and bit her lip thoughtfully. "Let's go back to the marina and try to find Talia and Zach. Maybe they can help us track down Rusty."

George nodded. "Sean said Zach was supposed to check back in at the *Lady Jane* by noon," she said.

Nancy glanced at her watch. "Then he should be there by now," she said. "Let's get going."

Nancy, Bess and George returned to their car. As Nancy opened the door on the driver's side, she noticed light bouncing off the roof of a nearby building onto the car. Glancing quickly at the roof, she thought she saw someone standing there.

Nancy sat down in her seat and pulled a mirrored compact from her purse. "I'm trying to see something," she explained. She angled the mirror to reflect the roof while pretending to put on lipstick. "Just keep talking," she said to her friends. "It's the bearded guy again, Bess," she finally announced. "He's watching us through a pair of binoculars."

"What bearded guy?" George asked.

Nancy filled George in on how she and Bess had been followed from the museum. "I got so caught up in the theft of the ingot, I completely forgot to tell you about it," Nancy said.

"That guy gives me the creeps," Bess said. "What do you think he wants?"

"I don't know, but I plan to find out," Nancy said with determination. She snapped her compact shut. "He's disappeared from the roof, and I bet anything he's heading for his car to follow us."

"Then let's get going before he can find us!" Bess fretted.

Nancy shook her head. "I want him to follow us back to the marina," she said. "Then maybe we can turn the tables on him and find out what he's up to."

As Nancy predicted, the bearded man's gray sedan soon appeared at the end of the street behind them. "There he is," Nancy said. "Here we go!"

She drove directly to the marina, with the sedan following at a discreet distance. "Now," she said after parking the car, "let's wander around some shops and see what he does."

"All right," Bess reluctantly agreed. "But for once I won't be able to concentrate on shopping."

The three girls got out of the car and headed for a cluster of shops at the edge of the marina.

With George and Bess following her lead, Nancy paused in front of a shop that sold tourist trinkets and souvenirs. They spent a moment checking out the window before ducking inside.

"Okay," Nancy whispered as soon as they were inside the shop. "Hide and wait to see what happens." Nancy ducked behind a post. George and Bess headed for the rear of the shop.

A minute later the bearded man appeared inside the shop. After a few more moments Nancy stepped out from behind the post and confronted him. "I'd like a word with you," she demanded in a loud voice.

Startled, the man whirled around and burst back out through the front door of the shop.

"Wait!" Nancy cried, sprinting after him. The man continued running toward the far end of the marina, where Hank's diving shop was located. He vanished inside the shop.

Nancy was about twenty steps behind him. She ran through the front door and crashed straight into Hank.

"If you're after that bearded guy, he just blew through here and out the back door," Hank said, trying to catch his breath.

Nancy took off with Hank right behind her. They ran out the back door and into an alley. The bearded man seemed to have vanished.

"Who was that guy, anyway?" Hank asked.

"I'd like to know that myself," Nancy said,

disappointed that the man had given her the slip. "Do you recall ever seeing him before, Hank?"

The shopkeeper shook his head. "No, I don't think so— Wait a minute," he said, stroking his chin thoughtfully. "I *do* remember seeing someone like him on a boat around here, though. I think it was the *Sea Scorpion.*"

"The *Sea Scorpion*—that's Leif Dorning's boat," Nancy said.

Nancy and Hank walked back inside the store. Hank reached for a rag to wipe his hands on. "By the way," he added, "I heard about Sean's gold ingot getting stolen."

When Nancy nodded, Hank continued, "I hear that Sean suspects Rusty stole it." He clucked his tongue disapprovingly. "I know Rusty's been having financial problems," he said. "It's a shame. He was quite a diver back when he worked for Dorning."

"Rusty worked for Leif Dorning?" Nancy's voice rose with her question. "I thought he worked for Sean."

"He worked for *both* of them, off and on," Hank shrugged. "When you're a treasure diver, you go where the money is," he explained.

So there's a connection between Rusty and Sean's rival, Nancy thought to herself. That meant it was possible that Dorning knew where the gold ingot was kept.

Nancy thanked Hank for his help. Then she

went back to the store to look for Bess and George, but they weren't there. Nancy decided to head back to the *Lady Jane,* hoping that her friends were there and that Rusty had turned up.

When Nancy reached the boat, she found everyone except Sean seated in the lounge cabin. They were eating sandwiches and talking about the gold ingot.

"I still can't believe that Rusty would do such a thing," Talia was saying to Bess. "He's cranky, but I always thought he had a good heart."

As soon as Nancy entered the lounge, Bess and George drew her aside. "What happened with the bearded guy, Nan?" George whispered. "We tried to follow, but we lost you."

Nancy filled them in on everything, including what Hank had said about seeing the bearded man on Leif Dorning's ship. "I also found out that Rusty once worked for Dorning," she said.

"Leif Dorning! The skipper who was giving Sean a hard time yesterday?" Bess asked.

Nancy nodded. "I think we have to investigate his role in all this."

Talia came up to them with a platter of sandwiches. Nancy suddenly realized she was very hungry. "Thanks, Talia," she said.

Just then the *Lady Jane*'s ship-to-shore phone rang. Zach answered it.

"Hi, Sean," Nancy heard him say. Then his face grew sober. "Okay, I'll put her on." He held the phone out to Nancy. "It's Sean—he sounds very upset."

Nancy sprang for the phone. "Sean, what's going on? Did you find Rusty?" she asked.

"I guess you could say that." Sean's voice sounded low and strained. "Rusty's dead."

"Dead?" A feeling of dread tightened in Nancy's stomach. "Sean, what happened?"

"He's been killed," Sean answered in a flat voice. "I'm at the Key West police station. Nancy, they think *I* murdered Rusty!"

Chapter

Five

Nancy squeezed her eyes shut as she tried to take in Sean's news. Rusty was dead, and Sean was accused of his murder!

"What happened, Sean?" Nancy asked at last, her voice full of concern. She was aware of the others looking at her with worried expressions.

"When I found Rusty finally, he was dead—stabbed. The police think I did it." Sean's explanation tumbled out in a rush.

Nancy tried to focus on what needed to be done next. "You can tell me the details when I see you. Right now it's very important that you call your lawyer."

"She's already here," Sean told Nancy. "I called her first. She's with the judge right now, arranging for my bail."

"That's good." Nancy tried to sound reassuring. "We'll come to the station right away to pick you up."

"Thanks," Sean said. Nancy could hear the slight catch in his voice. "I can't understand how this happened," he added weakly.

"Everything's going to be okay, Sean," Nancy said with more confidence than she felt.

"Nancy, what happened to Sean?" George said anxiously as Nancy hung up the phone. "I got the impression he's been arrested."

"He has—for the murder of Rusty Jones," Nancy said.

"Murder!" Talia exclaimed. "Poor Rusty! What happened? I mean, Sean wouldn't have—"

"Murdered Rusty?" Zach completed Talia's sentence. He shook his head firmly. "Sean wouldn't kill anyone."

"Of course he wouldn't." Talia looked at Nancy. "What can we do to help?"

"Just stay here while George and I go pick him up," Nancy said. "I'm sure we'll find out everything that's happened to him soon." She looked uncertainly at Bess. "George and I should probably just go by ourselves, Bess. Sean may not feel up to seeing too many people right now."

"Don't worry about me," Bess said quickly. "I'll be right here when you get back."

Ten minutes later Nancy was parking in front of the Key West Police Department. It was just about three o'clock. She and George jumped out of the car and hurried across the street to the tiny police station. Nancy smiled to see that the station was painted robin's egg blue.

Inside, they spotted Sean sitting on a plain wooden bench in the lobby. He was going over some papers with a young woman dressed in a tailored linen suit. Sean's face was worn and haggard.

"Sean!" George cried out. The young man's eyes lit up when he spotted her and Nancy.

"Hi, there." Sean reached up and squeezed George's hand. "I'm so glad you're here. George, Nancy, this is my attorney, Karen Miller. She's already posted my bail, so I'm free to go—for the moment."

"Sean told me all about you, Nancy," Karen said, shaking hands. "We may need your help to get Sean out of this mess."

"Tell me exactly what happened," Nancy urged.

Karen glanced around at the other people waiting in the lobby. "Let's step outside so we can talk privately," she suggested.

The four of them headed for a small park that was next door to the station.

"How serious is the evidence against Sean?" Nancy asked after they were seated on a stone bench.

"Very serious, I'm afraid," Karen said. "Tell her what happened, Sean."

Sean sighed. "When I left you guys to look for Rusty, I found a note on my windshield. It was from Rusty. He asked me to meet him at a boat house on the south side of the island."

"Did you go by yourself?" Nancy asked.

Sean nodded. "I know I should have let someone know where I was going—but I was too impatient to confront Rusty," he admitted.

"Then what happened?" George asked.

"When I got to the boat house, I thought it was deserted. There was a door on the side that was open, so I went in. It was very dark, and almost immediately I stumbled over something," Sean said. "It was Rusty's body." He shuddered. "I was so shocked, I couldn't think straight. I reached down to feel if he was still breathing. He wasn't, of course. That's when I felt some kind of metal rod lying next to him. I picked it up and took it outside to check it out. In the sunlight I saw that it was a fishing spear."

"A fishing spear!" George repeated. "What was that doing in the boat house?"

"It was the murder weapon," Nancy guessed.

"Yes," Karen answered.

"That means your fingerprints are all over it," Nancy commented. She tried not to sound as distressed as she felt.

Sean nodded miserably. "I dropped the spear when I saw what it was and flagged down a passing patrol car. They asked me a lot of questions, of course. After I mentioned the stolen ingot and how mad I was at Rusty, they brought me to the station."

Nancy sat quietly for a moment, thinking about how serious Sean's situation was. Finally she spoke. "This whole thing sounds like a setup to me. Sean, I'm wondering if you were intentionally framed, or whether Rusty really *did* want to speak with you, leading you to stumble onto the murder scene."

"That brings up the question of *why* Rusty was killed," Karen added.

Nancy nodded. "I'd like to see the note from Rusty that you found on your windshield," she said to Sean.

Karen pulled a paper out of her briefcase. "This is a photocopy of the note I turned over to the police."

Nancy studied the handwriting on the note, which was a heavy scrawl. "Is this Rusty's handwriting?" she asked Sean.

He held the note up. "No," he said with a heavy sigh. "Now that I think about it, Rusty always printed in block letters. I guess I was on such a tear, I didn't even notice the handwriting."

"Then I'd say somebody definitely tried to set you up for his murder," Nancy said. "Can you think of anyone whose handwriting matches this note—say, anyone on your crew?"

Sean shook his head. "I can't really remember," he said. He seemed to be on the verge of collapse.

"Don't worry about it right now." Nancy turned to Karen then. "I'd like a copy of this note, if you don't mind."

"Keep that one," Karen told her. "I have another in my briefcase. The fact that the handwriting isn't Rusty's should help Sean's case." She turned to face Nancy. "I'd appreciate any information you dig up about the real murderer, Nancy," she said. "The police feel they have their suspect, so they might not be motivated to look any further. Meanwhile, I'll use a connection I have in Miami to help with the case."

Nancy suddenly remembered that she hadn't told Sean about the mysterious bearded man who had followed her that day.

Sean shook his head when Nancy described the man. "Your description doesn't ring a bell at all," he said. "I can't imagine who he is—but I'll bet he's working with whoever's trying to frame me."

"Don't worry, Sean. Nancy will figure it out," George said, patting Sean's hand.

Karen rose to her feet. She reached into her purse and handed Nancy her card. "You can reach me at this number," she said.

"Thanks for bailing me out, Karen," Sean said grimly. "I'll repay you in gold as soon as we find the *Ninfa Marina*."

"Don't worry about it, Sean." Karen smiled slightly. "I'll talk to you tomorrow about the arraignment."

After Karen had left, Nancy, Sean, and George headed for the car. "I'm not sure where to go from here," Sean said dispiritedly.

"You've been through enough for one day," Nancy said firmly. "We'll drop you at your car so you can go home and get some rest."

"Rest—that sounds great." Sean rubbed his eyes wearily. "It feels like it's been about ten years since I got up this morning."

Nancy and George dropped Sean at the boat house, where he'd left his car. The doorway to the boat house was crisscrossed with the yellow police tape that marks off a crime scene. "I guess we'll have to postpone our dinner until tomorrow night, George," Sean said. "I think I'm just going to cook a frozen pizza, then fall into bed."

"Don't worry about it, Sean," George said softly.

Sean turned to Nancy. "I'll call Zach to tell him what happened. I'll also tell him to get the *Lady Jane* ready to go at dawn tomorrow," he said. "I'm determined to continue my search for the *Ninfa Marina,* despite all of this," he said. "I have a gut feeling that all this is being caused by someone who doesn't want me to find the treasure. I'm not about to back down, though!"

"Speaking of someone who doesn't want you

to find the treasure," Nancy said, "I want to check out Leif Dorning and his boat. Where can I find it?"

Sean gave her directions to the marina where the *Sea Scorpion* was anchored. After saying goodbye to Sean, Nancy and George drove back to the King Point Marina to pick up Bess. They found her sitting by herself on the deck of the *Lady Jane*.

"Thank goodness Sean didn't have to spend the night in jail," Bess said after Nancy finished filling her in on the details of his arrest. "That would have been the pits!"

"Where is everybody?" Nancy asked Bess. Zach and Talia were nowhere in sight.

"Zach just talked to Sean on the phone," Bess told them. "Then he went to pick up some supplies before Hank's store closes."

"What about Talia?" Nancy asked. "Where'd she go?"

"I don't know," Bess said, puzzled. "She got a phone call and left in a hurry." Bess peered down at her shoulder, which was now a bright pink. She touched it with her finger. "Ouch!" she said. "I guess I overdid it in the sun today."

"Where to now—the *Sea Scorpion,* as you told Sean?" George asked Nancy.

Nancy nodded and herded her friends back to the car. "I have a couple of good reasons for checking out Leif Dorning. He and Sean are bitter rivals. I also found out from Hank Morley that the bearded guy had been seen on his ship. This all makes me think that Dorning might be up to something," she said, nosing the car out of the parking lot.

"Maybe Dorning was working with Rusty and they got in a fight over the gold ingot." George conjectured.

"Good possibility, George," Nancy said. She frowned thoughtfully. "If Dorning *is* involved, he'd have to have an accomplice on the *Lady Jane* to set the fire and all. Maybe that's where Rusty came in." She paused. "On the other hand, maybe Rusty stole the ingot by himself, and someone found out about it—someone ready to kill him to get it.

"Well, we've got to start somewhere," Nancy said. "And Dorning's ship is as good a place as any. Who knows? Maybe we'll see the bearded guy there."

Nancy followed Sean's directions to the large commercial marina where the *Sea Scorpion* was docked. She spotted the sleek black boat tied up to one of the slips right away.

"I just want to look over the ship for now," Nancy explained to George and Bess. "I may need to search it for evidence later, but not now."

The three friends got out of the car and sat at a

dockside café. After ordering a light dinner, they surveyed the *Sea Scorpion*. Leif Dorning was having dinner with someone out on the deck.

All at once Nancy sat bolt upright. "You guys, look who's with Dorning!"

"I can't believe it," George said.

Dorning's dinner guest was Talia Ortiz!

Chapter

Six

"T<small>ALIA</small>?" George gasped out loud. "What's she doing having dinner with that creep Dorning?"

"I don't know, but I plan to find out," Nancy said. As they watched, Dorning leaned across the table and handed Talia a bulky white envelope.

"What's he giving her?" Bess whispered, biting into her fish sandwich. "Money, do you think?"

Deep in thought, Nancy only shrugged. "Tomorrow I'll have to find a way to get on board the *Sea Scorpion*," she finally said, ticking the points of her plan off on her fingers. "I also have to start investigating Talia. And at some point I need to talk to the police to find out whether they did an autopsy on Rusty's body."

A message was waiting for Nancy at the desk when they got back to the inn.

"Ned called to say hi," Nancy said softly, reading the note. It hit her again how much she missed him.

There was no answer when Nancy called him back, and she tried to hide her disappointment from her friends.

Bess understood Nancy's long face. "I'm sorry, Nan," she said soothingly. "I'm sure you'll be able to talk to him soon."

"Thanks, Bess." Nancy managed a smile. "I just was thinking again how much I wish he'd been able to come with us on this vacation," she said, and slowly climbed the stairs to their room.

At six the next morning, Nancy and George arrived at the *Lady Jane*.

"Hi, girls," Sean said, greeting them on deck. He looked better than he had the day before, but he was still subdued. "Where's Bess?" he asked.

"She got a little overdone in the sun yesterday," Nancy explained. "So she's staying inside today."

"Oh, that's too bad," Sean said. Just then Zach and Talia appeared up on the deck.

"Let's get her under way," Sean said to the first mate.

Zach silently turned and made his way to the pilothouse with the characteristic rolling walk of a man who made his living on a boat. Talia nodded at Nancy and George before moving off to the bow.

Everyone's spirits were low, Nancy observed. The death of their friend and mate had cast a pall over the treasure-hunting expedition.

After proceeding slowly out of the harbor, the *Lady Jane* surged forward in open waters. Once they were safely under way Nancy sought out Talia to press her about her meeting with Leif Dorning. She found the marine archaeologist out on the forward deck, mixing some goopy liquid in a pail.

"What's that?" Nancy asked, kneeling beside her.

Talia stirred the stuff with a stick. "It's a waterproof polymer we use for preserving underwater artifacts," she explained. "This allows us to remove items we find without disturbing them."

"I remember yesterday Sean said that Leif Dorning was a blow-and-go kind of treasure hunter," she said. "What does that mean?"

Talia dropped her eyes. "Dorning used to be notorious for destroying coral beds and fish habitats while he was treasure hunting, but I think he's changing his ways," she said carefully.

Nancy couldn't read Talia's attitude toward Dorning, and before she had time to ask any more questions, Sean tapped her on the shoulder.

"Come with me, you two," he said excitedly. "I want to show you something interesting on the subbottom profiler."

Nancy had meant to tell Sean about Talia's meeting with Dorning, but she forgot in the excitement of the moment. She and Talia followed him to the pilothouse, where George and Zach were monitoring a small screen that resembled a video game.

"This machine shows us an outline of what's underneath us," Sean explained.

"Look, you can see a school of fish passing right below the boat," he said, pointing to a group of moving white flecks.

Next Sean drew their attention to a large object on the ocean floor. Its curved outline resembled a ship. "That's what we want to check out," he said. "It could just be a bed of coral, or it *could* be a ship. I have extra wet suits and tanks for you girls. George says you're both accomplished and certified divers."

Nancy shook her head. "I think I'll sit this one out," she said, noticing George throw her a surprised look. "I'm feeling a little seasick," she fibbed.

George drew Nancy aside. "What's going on, Nancy? You *never* get seasick," she whispered.

"I know," Nancy replied under her breath. "I want to check out Talia's things while she's underwater."

George, Sean, and Talia put on their wetsuits, air tanks with regulators attached to vests with buoyancy-control devices, and masks. Nancy helped them with the equipment, which was very heavy on land. Then the three crawled over the side of the boat and fell into the water.

As soon as the divers had disappeared below the surface, Nancy looked for Zach. He was nowhere in sight.

She slipped quietly into the main cabin and searched. Opening a series of storage bins, she soon found what she wanted—Talia's boat bag. Inside the bag were Talia's wallet, sunscreen, and a change of clothes.

Nancy plucked out the wallet and flipped it open. A folded paper fluttered to the floor. It was a letter that Talia was writing to her mother.

I know I should be more forgiving, but I hold Sean responsible for Jaime's death. He should have known that Jaime was too inexperienced for such a hazardous dive. Sometimes I wish Sean would suffer for what he did—the way we have!

Mentally, Nancy compared Talia's letter with the note Sean had found on his windshield the day before. Talia's delicate script did not match the heavy scrawl on Sean's note, though Nancy knew that whoever had written the note could have disguised his or her handwriting.

Just then a sudden noise right behind Nancy startled her, and she hastily replaced Talia's letter and shoved the boat bag back into its storage bin.

"Are you feeling better?" Zach had seemed to materialize out of thin air.

Nancy bent over and pretended to be tying one of her sneakers. "Much better, thanks," she said.

"It's better to stay topside in the fresh air if you're feeling seasick," he said slowly, appraising her.

"Thanks, I'll do that," Nancy said. She brushed past him, hoping that he hadn't seen her going through Talia's things.

Nancy seated herself in a deck chair to get some sun and think. It was clear that Talia blamed Sean for her brother's death. Could her bitterness have driven her to work with Leif Dorning? Nancy wondered. If so, could Talia be the one sabotaging Sean and his hunt for the *Ninfa Marina*? She might even be linked to Rusty's murder because it was possible that the cook had been working with Talia and Leif Dorning. Perhaps they had a falling out over the stolen gold ingot, and he was killed during a quarrel. They could have set up Sean as the murderer to clear themselves.

There was a great rushing sound, and Nancy

saw the bubbles that preceded Sean and the other divers to the surface. A few seconds later they broke the surface, and Sean lifted up his mask. His expression reflected his frustration.

"It was just a big mound of coral," he said. "But we'll keep searching. My research makes me positive the *Ninfa Marina* went down right around here."

After boarding the *Lady Jane,* Talia attached a box-shaped gadget to a towline and dropped it into the water behind the *Lady Jane.*

"This is the proton magnetometer," Talia explained. "It will give out a signal if we pass over anything large and metallic—like a ship's cannon, or even the treasure itself."

They spent the next two hours trolling with the proton magnetometer. During that time Nancy caught Sean alone. "I need to talk to you, Sean." She wanted to tell him about Talia's meeting with Leif Dorning and the letter she'd found, but before she could say anything more, she was interrupted by a wild clacking. The noise was coming from the proton magnetometer that Talia was monitoring.

"We've got something big and metallic, right under us, Sean!" Talia shouted in an excited voice.

"Sure doesn't seem like a mound of coral this time," Sean said. "Let's check it out on the profiler."

59

He ran into the pilothouse, followed by Nancy. Everyone was clustered around the subbottom profiler, which indicated that there was another large object directly beneath the boat.

"Let's go down and check it out," Sean said.

"If you have one more suit, I'll go with you this time," Nancy said, picking up on the excitement. They all hurriedly got ready. After double-checking their air tanks and buoyancy-control devices, the four divers plunged into the ocean.

Four white trails of bubbles rose up from them as they descended through the crystalline depths.

Nancy breathed steadily through her regulator. It felt great to be diving again. The ocean was surprisingly shallow, even this far out from land. Nancy thought it was only about forty feet deep at the most. Shafts of sunlight pierced the water all the way down to the ocean floor.

Below them, Nancy could just make out something large and dark resting on the sandy bottom. Her heart skipped a beat.

Once on the bottom she could see that the object was a long and rusty chain lying on the sand. The chain was tangled around a hill of boulders and rocks. At the end of the chain lay an old ship's anchor.

Talia and Sean quickly swam forward to inspect the anchor up close. Nancy and George watched as they gently scraped away algae and residue that had built up on the anchor.

Sean pointed excitedly at the area he had just finished cleaning. The spot was imprinted with the letters *N.M.*—for *Ninfa Marina!*

The divers gave one another slow high fives and exchanged smiles behind their masks and regulators. The *Ninfa Marina*—or part of it, at least—had been found!

After a few moments to savor their find, Sean and Talia started to search the immediate area for the treasure. After half an hour with no luck, Talia signaled that she was going around to check the far side of the rock pile. Kicking away from the heavy anchor, she immediately disappeared behind the rocks.

Nancy gazed around. Although there was fairly good light, she decided to use her flashlight to probe the dark crevices of the rocky pile in front of her. Out of the corner of her eye, she saw that George and Sean were about ten yards off to her right, using small brushes to sweep back the layers of sand around the anchor.

Nancy was swimming around a large boulder at the base of the rock pile when she heard and felt a low rumbling. Raising her head, she became terrified by what she saw. A cluster of large rocks had dislodged themselves from the pile just above her. The boulders were tumbling straight at her—she was about to be buried by an undersea avalanche!

Chapter
Seven

NANCY KNEW she had just seconds before she would be crushed by the falling rocks.

Summoning all her strength, she kicked back powerfully with her legs. A tumbling rock missed her by a fraction of an inch as she shot out from under the path of the avalanche. The boulders landed with sickening thuds onto the ocean floor, throwing up a cloud of sandy debris.

As soon as she knew she was out of danger, Nancy hung suspended in the water and drew in shaky gulps of air through the regulator. I'm lucky to be alive, she thought, her pulse racing from the near-miss.

George and Sean quickly swam to her side. George tapped her, indicating her concern. Nancy nodded that she was all right and gave the thumbs-up sign.

Talia reappeared then from the other side of the rock pile. The marine archaeologist seemed to be shaken by what had happened. Sean signaled for them all to return to the surface and sunlight. They rose slowly and made sure they breathed the whole way up to prevent air embolisms.

"It was just an accident," Nancy insisted again to Zach when she was on board the boat. "No person could have triggered it, and I just can't believe that an avalanche could be caused by a curse."

"Maybe you should start believing in curses," Zach muttered darkly. His usually impassive face was agitated. "I know it sounds nuts, but look what's happened since we started searching for the *Ninfa Marina*. First Jaime was killed, then we had all those accidents, and then Rusty was murdered," he said. "Not to mention that you nearly got crushed in a rock slide."

Nancy was sitting with Zach and the others around the galley table. They were huddled over bowls of steaming soup and thick slices of bread and were discussing Nancy's close call.

"Talia, did you see any sign that the rocks were about to tumble?" Nancy asked the marine archaeologist, who had been on the far side of the rock pile when the avalanche occurred.

Talia shook her head. "I didn't realize what

63

was happening until I heard that horrible rumbling. It sounded like an earthquake." She shuddered. "As I was swimming back, I was terrified that I'd find you all crushed."

For a brief moment Nancy wondered whether Talia could somehow have rigged the avalanche. She banished the thought almost immediately—it would have taken superhuman strength to topple those boulders.

Nancy decided to change the subject. "So we've found the *Ninfa Marina*'s anchor, but about the treasure?" she asked. "Do you think we'll find it as well?"

"Absolutely," Sean said with a spark of his old enthusiasm. "It may take a while, though." He bit into a piece of buttered bread and stared at the others with a serious expression. "Let's keep a tight lid on the news. I don't want Dorning muscling in on this while we're still searching for the treasure. I've noted the location of the anchor in the log so we can continue our search tomorrow in the right place."

"So you do expect to find the treasure nearby?" Nancy asked Sean.

Talia shook her head. "The treasure from these old ships is rarely in one spot—the years and currents spread it over many miles," she explained. "But the fact that we found the anchor means we're getting closer to the mother lode."

"Mother lode?" George echoed. "What's that?"

"It's the pot of gold at the end of the rainbow," Zach said softly. He leaned back and folded his arms behind his head. "The main pile of treasure —chests of gold and silver bars and chains. It's what every treasure diver spends his life dreaming about."

"What happens *after* you find the treasure?" Nancy asked, taking a sip of her soup. "Do you share it?"

"Some get more than others," Zach snapped, glowering at Sean. "Most of us work for pennies and promises." He rose from the table. "I've got work to do," he said, and headed for the companionway that led up to the deck.

"What was that about?" Nancy asked in the silence that followed his exit.

Sean shifted uncomfortably. "Zach feels he's entitled to a larger share of the treasure than I've promised him," he said. "The lion's share of it will go to taxes and the investors. I couldn't afford to give him a bigger share, even if I wanted to." He heaved a sigh, and Nancy knew that the pressure of the past couple of days was weighing heavily on him.

George reached over and playfully shook Sean's shoulder. "Come on, Mr. Mahoney," she said, stacking the dirty bowls. "Let's drown our troubles in a sink of soapy dishwater."

"You've got a deal," Sean said, managing a grin.

While he and George started clearing the table, Nancy turned the case over in her mind. Zach's outburst made her think. Perhaps she shouldn't be concentrating wholly on Talia as a suspect. It was obvious now that Zach had his own ax to grind when it came to Sean.

She stood up abruptly and joined George and Sean at the sink. "I'll give you a hand with the drying," she said, grabbing a towel. She continued drying dishes until she saw Talia get up and head topside. "I'd like to look through Zach's things," she said quietly to Sean.

"Why?" he asked in a surprised tone.

"He was pretty upset when he left the table," Nancy explained. "It just makes sense to check him out."

Sean shook his head. "Zach's an old buddy of mine from way back—I don't think he could be involved in any of this," he said. Then he shrugged. "But if you insist . . ." He tried unsuccessfully to open a nearby storage cabinet. "I guess he locked his stuff up today. He doesn't usually do that," Sean said, puzzled. He reached in his pocket and dug out a small silver key. "Fortunately, my master key opens everything on board."

"Thanks," Nancy replied, glancing back to make sure they were still alone.

Sean understood her concern. "George and I will go up top and make sure Talia and Zach are kept busy," he told her.

As soon as she was alone in the galley, Nancy unlocked Zach's locker and rummaged through his things. She found a "To Do" list that the mate had written and could see right away that Zach's handwriting didn't match that on Sean's note.

Nancy kept searching. The only unusual item she found was a paperback stuffed into the bottom of his boat bag. It was a book of ghost stories. Zach obviously was a believer when it came to the supernatural, Nancy thought to herself. She relocked the locker with a sigh. If Zach had anything to do with Rusty's murder or the sabotage of Sean's boat, the evidence was not there.

Nancy felt the cabin vibrate as the *Lady Jane*'s engines were revved up. Sean popped his head into the galley. "We're heading back to the marina," he announced. "I want to stay out here and keep searching for the treasure, but I have to meet with my lawyer." He lowered his voice. "Did you find anything incriminating in Zach's locker?" he whispered.

Nancy shook her head. Then she remembered that she hadn't told him about her suspicions regarding Talia Ortiz. Quickly Nancy described Talia's meeting with Leif Dorning, and the letter in which she blamed Sean for her brother's death.

Sean's face sagged. "I'm not surprised that Talia blames me for Jaime's death," he said. "I blame myself. I should have *triple*-checked those air tanks that day. But I *am* surprised by her meeting with Dorning," he continued with an angry edge to his voice. "I wonder if she's spilled any confidential information about our expedition."

"It's possible," Nancy replied, "which makes her the likely sabotage suspect. Who knows? If Dorning is the one trying to frame you for Rusty's murder, she might have helped him with that, too."

Sean narrowed his green eyes. "I can't believe that Talia would be involved in something like that."

"I hope I'm wrong," Nancy said quickly. "In any case, I need to gather more evidence before we can confront her with any of this."

Just then George appeared behind Sean. "Take a break, you two," she said, grinning. "Come up top. It's a glorious day to be out on the water!"

Nancy accompanied George and Sean topside. George was right—it *was* a spectacular afternoon. The ocean was blue and calm, broken only by the thinnest whitecaps. A family of dolphins followed them most of the way back to the marina, frolicking playfully as they arched across the *Lady Jane's* wake.

Nancy leaned against the railing and watched, enthralled.

As they pulled into the marina, Nancy spotted Bess standing on the dock, waving to them. A tall, well-built guy was standing next to her. Something about him was very familiar to Nancy. When she looked at him again, her heart soared. It was Ned!

Nancy was the first person off the boat. She practically flew onto the dock and into Ned's waiting arms.

"Hey, Drew," Ned whispered into her ear. "I couldn't stay away from you, it turns out." He held her tightly against him.

Nancy buried her face in Ned's shoulder. She was so happy to see him it made her knees weak. "I'm glad to see you, Ned," she finally managed to whisper.

"Is that all you can say?" Ned asked teasingly. He gently lifted her face toward his, and then their lips melted together in a long, sizzling kiss.

"You have no idea how hard it was for me not to spill the beans about Ned's coming!" Bess giggled. "Ned and I have been plotting this since before we left River Heights. Thank goodness I had my sunburn to use as an excuse, so I could stay behind and pick him up at the Key West airport."

"You took a puddle jumper from Miami?" Nancy asked Ned.

He nodded. "I only have a few days off, so I wanted to get here as fast as possible," he explained. "Bess drove me straight here from the airport and explained that you've taken on a new case."

By now everyone was clustered together on the dock. Nancy introduced Ned to Sean and the crew. "I'll go to the hotel with you, Ned. Then I'm afraid I've got a couple of things to take care of before dinner," Nancy said, remembering her plan to check out the *Sea Scorpion*.

Sean drew her aside. "Take the afternoon off, Nancy," he said quietly. "You've been working hard ever since you got here. I insist you cool it for a little while."

"That's right, Nancy." George grinned. "That will give Sean the perfect excuse to take a break, too, after he talks to his lawyer."

Sean smiled into George's eyes. "We'll take that walk on the beach I've been promising you."

Bess smiled and patted her pocketbook. "I've been itching to do a little shopping in Mallory Square," she said. "One of our guidebooks says it's the place to buy fabulous hand-printed skirts. I plan to blow a bundle," she added mischievously.

"I guess that settles it," Nancy said to Ned. "We're on our own for a romantic afternoon."

"Sounds really great to me." Ned grinned.

After taking Bess to Mallory Square, Nancy and Ned went to the Sunset Cove Inn. Ned picked up his key from the desk, and he and Nancy took the stairs to his room on the second floor.

Ned opened the door and dropped his bags. "This is great," he said, nodding at the view. "I love being able to see the water."

They were interrupted by a loud knock on the door just then. Nancy opened it to find a food service cart sitting outside in the hallway.

"That's weird," Ned said, coming up behind her. "We didn't order anything. They must have brought it to the wrong room."

The tray on the serving cart was covered with a large metal warming cover. "I wonder why the waiter didn't wait to make sure we got this," he mused, lifting the lid.

Nancy gasped in horror. "Ned, look at that!" she exclaimed.

"Ugh!" he cried, dropping the lid. He and Nancy recoiled as they stared down at what lay on the plate.

Sitting on a bed of lettuce was a hideous human skull! Wedged between its teeth was a note. Gingerly Nancy removed the paper and read its message aloud.

"'Keep away from the *Ninfa Marina,*'" the note warned, "'or you'll be the next to die!'"

Chapter

Eight

Nancy sprinted down the hallway, trying to catch whoever had left the skull and note. Her pulse was racing from the shock.

Nancy reached the end of the hallway and peered down the stairwell. She managed to catch a glimpse of brown hair as the door at the bottom of the stairs was closing.

"Stop!" Nancy called after him. She flew down the steps, taking them two at a time with Ned right behind her.

When they reached the bottom, Nancy flung open the door and found herself standing in the gravel parking lot. A car engine roared to life off to her left. A moment later a gray sedan flew past her and peeled out of the parking lot, throwing up a spurt of gravel and dust. Nancy saw the driver—it was the mysterious bearded man.

Who *is* that guy? she wondered. She knew she had to find out.

Nancy turned to Ned.

"We lost him!" she muttered. "And the license plates were so muddy I couldn't get a number." Nancy knew the man had purposely smeared the plates with mud because they had been obliterated the day before, too.

"Lost who?" Ned asked. "Nancy, what's this all about? Does he have something to do with this new case?"

Nancy filled him in on the most recent developments. "The man we were chasing is the same person who followed me to the marina yesterday," Nancy said. "I don't know who he is, but I'm sure he's the one who left that skull outside your door."

Nancy and Ned returned to his room to inspect the skull that was still staring up from the serving tray.

"Obviously the bearded guy is trying to scare me off the case," Nancy said. "But why?" She walked into Ned's room and picked up the telephone.

"Who are you calling?" Ned wanted to know.

"Room service," Nancy replied, punching in some numbers. "I want to find out if anyone knew that cart was sent up here."

Nancy spoke briefly with the person in charge of room service before hanging up. She looked at

Ned. "They don't have any record of sending an order to this floor, but one of their carts is missing," she told him. "Our mystery man must have 'borrowed' it for his little errand."

Nancy then filled Ned in on the other suspects, including Leif Dorning, Talia Ortiz, and Zach Hardwick. "Our bearded man must be working with one of them, but I haven't been able to figure out how he fits into the whole picture."

"What do you want to do now?" Ned asked. "You aren't about to be scared off the case, are you?"

"No way." Nancy shook her head with determination. She peered at the note in her hands. "Wait a minute," she said. "This handwriting is the same heavy scrawl as that on Sean's note."

"What did Sean's note say?" Ned asked.

"Sean found it on his car the day Rusty was killed," Nancy explained. "It told him to meet Rusty at an old boat house. The same place, of course, where Rusty lay dead."

"So you think this bearded guy killed Rusty," Ned said, more worried now. "Nancy, he could be very dangerous."

"I know," Nancy said. "That's why it's important that we nab him as soon as possible."

"Well, I'm going to stick to you like glue," Ned said seriously. "Consider me your personal bodyguard until this is over."

"You know I can take care of myself, but I do love the attention." Nancy threw her arms around her boyfriend and gave him a big bear hug.

"What's the next step?" Ned asked.

"I've got to find a way to get on Leif Dorning's boat," Nancy said, checking her watch. "Hank Morley told me he saw the bearded man there. I need to find evidence linking Dorning to either the murder or the sabotage. I also need to confirm that Talia is his contact on the *Lady Jane.* It's very possible that Dorning is behind this whole thing. I do want to stop by Hank's place to see if he can remember anything else about the bearded guy that could help us."

At five o'clock Nancy and Ned pulled into the parking lot of the King Point Marina. She and Ned walked over to Hank Morley's diving and engine shop. They found Hank working in a metal shack beside the shop. He was soldering some wires on a small, cigar-shaped craft. It resembled the submersible on the *Lady Jane.*

Nancy introduced Ned to the shop owner, then asked, "Is that an underwater submersible, Hank?"

"Yeah," Hank said. "I'm repairing it for a big client." He patted the submersible's hull appreciatively. "I wish I could afford high-tech gear like this. My old tub's docked right there," he said, pointed to an aging wooden boat that was moored in the waterway just beyond the shop's front door. Hank lowered his voice. "You hear anything about Sean, Nancy? Have the police figured out who murdered Rusty? No one around here believes Sean did it."

"I don't know anything more than you do, I'm afraid," Nancy said carefully. She didn't want to go into details since she still wasn't sure who the culprit was. She also didn't want anybody else to find out that she was investigating.

"Poor Sean," Hank said. "I'd hate to see him go to jail for something he didn't do."

"Hank, I wanted to try to jog your memory about the bearded man who ran through your shop the other day," Nancy said. "Can you remember anything else about him—like when it was you last saw him on Dorning's ship? Could he have been a member of Dorning's crew?"

Hank thought for a moment. "I think I saw him there pretty recently," the shopkeeper said slowly. "But I can't say for sure." He paused for a minute to question Nancy. "Do you think that guy had something to do with Rusty's murder?"

"It's possible," Nancy replied quickly. She said goodbye to Hank and returned to the parking lot with Ned.

As soon as they got back in the car, Nancy turned to Ned. "Let's go to the marina where the

Sea Scorpion is anchored," she said. "Maybe I can figure out a way to get on board without being spotted."

They drove across the island to a large commercial marina. Nancy scoured the marina for the sleek black boat, but it was nowhere around.

"Dorning must have gone out for the day," Nancy said, stifling her disappointment. "We'll just wait until he comes back in."

"Now that we're here, we might as well order dinner even if it is early," Ned said, patting his stomach. "I'm really hungry. The lunch I got on the plane would've starved a bird."

"Good idea," Nancy agreed.

She and Ned took a table near the back of the dockside café so they wouldn't be noticed. Then they feasted on a wonderful meal of broiled sole and roasted potatoes.

They were still sitting and enjoying the view at sunset. As Nancy was finishing a cup of tea, she spotted the *Sea Scorpion* heading into port.

"There's the boat," Nancy announced triumphantly. They watched as Dorning and his two crew members quickly tied up the *Sea Scorpion*. Dorning locked the big sliding glass door that led into the ship's main cabin; then everyone disembarked.

Nancy scanned the crew, hoping to spot the bearded man, but he was nowhere in sight. She glanced at her watch. "Seven-thirty," she said. "They're probably done for the day. I just hope they'll stay gone long enough for me to check out the boat."

"How do you plan to get onto her?" Ned asked.

Nancy pulled out a leather pouch that contained her special lock-picking tools. "I never leave home without them." She grinned.

As soon as Dorning and his crew were gone, Nancy and Ned walked onto the dock as if they were tourists taking an after-dinner stroll. Nancy surveyed the *Sea Scorpion.* The sleek black ship was smaller than the *Lady Jane,* but it was outfitted with the same high tech treasure-hunting equipment. Nancy hoped there wasn't a high-tech alarm on board, as well.

Nancy turned to Ned. "Why don't you wait for me back on shore—I'll attract much less attention by myself," she said.

Ned nodded. "I'll move the car down by the last dock, so we can take off when you're done," he suggested.

"Good idea," Nancy replied, turning and strolling casually onto the *Sea Scorpion*'s deck.

Whipping out her lock-picking tools, Nancy quickly got the main door down to the cabins open. She waited a moment, then sighed—no alarm had sounded.

Nancy stepped boldly down the few steps into what appeared to be the galley. Several wooden doors led off the main cabin into smaller bunkrooms. Nancy opened doors until she found the main stateroom near the front of the ship. She figured it had to be Dorning's cabin.

Nancy briskly set about checking out Dorning's possessions. She peered at the walls, which were plastered with dozens of pictures of Dorning holding various trophies. He isn't exactly shy about his accomplishments, Nancy thought to herself. Her eye was drawn to one photo in particular. It was a picture of Dorning with Talia Ortiz. They were standing on the deck of the *Sea Scorpion*—entwined in an embrace!

Nancy stared at the picture for a long moment. This seemed to prove that Talia was involved with Leif Dorning, Nancy realized.

Suddenly she jerked her head around. There was a noise coming from the other side of the door. She opened the cabin door a sliver and peered out. Leif Dorning had just returned!

Through the cracked door, Nancy could see the tall, blond Dorning making his way through the main galley. He was heading straight for the cabin where Nancy was standing. She had to get out fast!

Moving swiftly, Nancy reached for a small porthole over Dorning's bunk. She struggled to open the porthole, but succeeded only in gnashing her teeth in frustration. The window was bolted from the outside.

Glancing around desperately, Nancy heard the door handle turn behind her. Any second now Dorning would come in and she'd be caught!

Chapter

Nine

THE LAST THING Nancy wanted was a confrontation with Dorning. Her eyes darted quickly about, and she spied the only possible avenue of escape—a narrow door on the far side of the cabin. It looked like a closet of some kind.

As Dorning entered the cabin, Nancy stole through the smaller door and found herself in a cramped storage room. She froze for a moment, scarcely daring to breathe as Dorning moved about in the room outside.

After what seemed an eternity, Nancy heard Dorning leave the cabin. Now she had to find a way out. She didn't dare escape the way she'd come in because Dorning was probably still on board.

Nancy felt a draft from somewhere overhead

and looked up to find a hatch in the ceiling. Nancy hoped it led directly up onto the deck. Taking a deep breath, she carefully slid back the bolt and lifted herself onto the deck.

"Hey, you!" a man yelled from the dock.

Without pausing to check him out, Nancy made it to the edge of the deck in three quick strides. With a quick hop she dove smoothly over the side. There was barely a ripple as she knifed cleanly into the water.

Nancy swam underwater until her lungs were ready to burst. She knew she had to put as much distance as possible between herself and the *Sea Scorpion* before coming up for air.

She broke the surface just beyond the last dock. The first thing she saw was Ned's worried face.

He helped her out of the water and wrapped his sweater around her while she told him what had happened.

"Do you think you were recognized?" he asked.

"I'm not sure," Nancy said, shivering slightly. "But Dorning knows someone broke into his ship."

Ned hugged her to him. "You could have gotten hurt, Drew," he said in her ear. "How could you take such a risk?"

"It was worth it, Ned. I found something on board that makes Talia a major suspect."

"Let's get you warm and dry, then you can tell me all about it," Ned said protectively.

Nancy and Ned put up the top of the convertible and drove back to the inn, where they found George and Bess sitting on the front porch swing.

Bess's blue eyes widened when she caught sight of Nancy. "What happened to you?" she cried. "You're soaked!"

"I'm fine, really," Nancy replied. She kissed Ned good night and quickly told her friends about her close call on the *Sea Scorpion* as they went up to their room so she could change. "But before Leif Dorning almost caught me, I found a picture of him and Talia. I'm pretty sure they're dating."

"I can't believe she cares about that guy," Bess said, wrinkling her nose with distaste.

"That would give her a big reason to wreck Sean's treasure hunt," George said angrily.

"You're right, George." Nancy nodded as she dried her hair with a towel. "I already knew from Talia's letter that she blames Sean for her brother's death. Now it turns out she's dating his number-one rival. I think I should tell Sean about it right away."

"Sean just called a little while ago. Karen canceled their meeting earlier today so they're meeting tonight—probably until quite late," George said.

"He and Karen are probably planning his

83

defense," Nancy said. "I guess my news can keep until morning." George had a slightly wistful expression on her face, she noticed. "Tell me about your date," Nancy prodded, pulling her robe tighter around her.

"We just had a nice, quiet walk on the beach." George blushed. "I found some beautiful shells." She took a deep breath and turned her head away. "I'm just starting to realize how much I want everything to be okay for Sean," she added quietly.

"So do I, George," Nancy said. "So do I."

Nancy was up before the sun the next morning. She wanted to call Sean before he left for the *Lady Jane*.

"Hi, Nancy." Sean sounded dispirited. "Last night I found out that Karen managed to postpone my arraignment for a month. Unfortunately, I also found out that the police didn't turn up any fingerprints other than mine on the fishing spear that killed Rusty. And the autopsy showed that the spear definitely was the murder weapon. So it looks like I'm still the only suspect."

"I'm sorry to hear that, Sean," Nancy replied. "But we may be closing in on the real murderer. Last night I searched Leif Dorning's boat. I found a picture that proves he and Talia are going out."

There was a long silence on the other end of the

phone. "I'll bet anything Talia has told Dorning about the anchor we just found," he fumed.

"As a member of your crew, Talia had plenty of opportunities for sabotage," Nancy pointed out. "She and Dorning could be behind the whole thing—including Rusty's death. We know that Rusty used to work for Dorning. Maybe Rusty was in league with them and was killed during a quarrel over the gold ingot."

"I hate to think that Talia is really involved in all this," Sean said sadly.

"We'll have to confront her as soon as she arrives on board this morning," Nancy said.

"That sounds like a good idea," Sean replied. "Let's all meet at the *Lady Jane* in half an hour." Then he hung up.

Nancy pulled on a T-shirt and a pair of jeans, then waited for Bess and George to get ready. They picked up Ned and headed for the marina, skipping breakfast. As they stepped onto the *Lady Jane's* deck, Nancy saw that Sean was already on board with Zach. The two men were inside the pilothouse huddled over some charts.

"Where's Talia?" Nancy asked.

"She left a message on my machine saying she'd be a little late," Zach said.

Nancy decided not to refer to her conversation with Sean in front of Zach. She still hadn't ruled him out as a suspect.

Sean disappeared down into the galley and

soon reappeared on deck bearing a platter of doughnuts and two thermoses, one of tea and one of coffee.

"Mmm, look at those doughnuts," Bess said. "Who do we have to thank for these?"

"Me." Sean grinned. "I always start off the day on a full stomach."

"My sentiments exactly," Bess said. She picked up a powdered doughnut and took a bite.

Nancy was just reaching for a doughnut as a shadow fell across the group. She turned around and saw Leif Dorning standing on the dock.

Dorning stopped short when he saw Nancy. "You!" he yelled at her. "You broke into my ship last night, didn't you!"

So he did get a good look at me last night, Nancy realized uncomfortably. Before she had a chance to reply, Sean stepped forward. "Give it a rest, Dorning," he began, but Nancy interrupted him.

"I was on board the *Sea Scorpion* last night," she said, "investigating Rusty's murder." She took a step forward. "I have reason to suspect you may be involved in it as well as in the sabotage of the *Lady Jane*."

Dorning's jaw dropped. "I never did that old geezer any harm," he said defensively. "And speaking of sabotage, if we hadn't interrupted you last night, I'll bet you would have done something to the *Sea Scorpion.* And not for the first time, either!" he sputtered.

"Wait a minute," Nancy said, confused by the counterattack. Dorning had accused Sean of sabotaging him a couple of days earlier, too. "You're saying that the *Sea Scorpion* has been sabotaged, too?"

"You bet it has!" Dorning blustered. "Just last week someone poked a hole in our fuel line. I suspect you were behind it, Sean."

"I don't believe a word of this, Dorning," he snapped. "You're just blowing smoke to cover your own tracks."

Bess, Ned, and George had been listening off to the side. George shook her head. "What do you make of all this, Nan?" she asked.

"I'm not sure," Nancy said slowly. "It sounds as if someone may have it in for *both* Sean and Dorning."

"Leif! What are you doing here?"

Nancy whirled around and saw Talia approaching.

"I was just leaving," Dorning said, his eyes softening as he took in Talia.

Just then Nancy blurted out, "Tell me something, Dorning, have you ever had a tall, brown-haired man work on your boat—a man with a full beard and mustache?"

Dorning shook his head. "I don't know any

guys with full beards," he said. He looked from Nancy to Sean. "I don't know exactly what's going on, but I'm keeping my eye on you two," he said. "And stay off the *Sea Scorpion*. Next time I'll have you arrested!"

As Talia boarded, she looked anxiously at Sean. "Why did Leif come here?" she asked. "Is something wrong?"

"Something is definitely wrong," Sean snapped. "When did you and Dorning start seeing each other?"

Talia flushed a bright red. "Leif was very kind to me after my brother died," she explained, setting down her boat bag. "He—he sent me a very sweet sympathy note. After that we started talking once in a while." She twisted a friendship ring on her finger.

"Why didn't you tell Sean about your relationship with Dorning?" Nancy asked her.

"I didn't think Sean would understand—I know he and Leif can't stand each other," she said with a sigh. "Leif's really a good person underneath all that bluster," she explained to Nancy. "He's become quite conscious of protecting the environment when he treasure hunts now."

"I'm just curious to know about your dinner meeting with Dorning the other night on his boat," Nancy said. "What was it he gave you in the big white envelope?"

Talia seemed to be puzzled for a moment. Then she smiled. "Oh, just some articles I lent him about the environment."

Nancy nodded but felt doubtful. She wanted to believe that Dorning and Talia were telling the truth, but she couldn't ignore the possibility that they were both lying.

Nancy looked at Sean. "I want to talk to Hank Morley again," she said. "He's the one who told me about seeing the bearded man on board the *Sea Scorpion.* Maybe he was mistaken." She glanced at her watch—it was still only seven-thirty. "Do you think Hank's open this early?" she asked.

"Sure," Zach spoke up. "I'll go with you. I need to get our air tanks filled up, anyway."

"George, maybe you and Bess can give me a hand getting the galley ready this morning," Sean said. "With Rusty gone, things are kind of a mess."

"Sure thing," George said, nodding.

"Kitchen work—my least favorite," Bess groaned quietly into Nancy's ear as she and George followed Sean down to the galley.

Nancy, Ned, and Zach carried the air tanks to Hank's shop. Nancy found Hank working behind the cash register.

"Hi, Hank," Nancy said, greeting him. "Remember when you said you thought you saw that guy we chased through your shop on board the *Sea Scorpion*. Leif Dorning says he doesn't know anyone who fits that description. Do you think it could have been another boat you were thinking about?"

Morley scratched his head. "Could be," he said slowly. "But I was sure it was Dorning's." He shrugged. "Maybe my memory's not what it used to be."

Zach came out from the back of the shop with Ned. "Hey, Hank," he said. "Your air tank pump is busted. I'll have to go all the way to Diver Dan's to fill these tanks." He checked his watch and grimaced. "I really need to get back to the boat to help Sean map out a course for our trip today."

"Nancy and I could get the tanks filled," Ned volunteered.

Zach smiled. "That'd be great," he said. Zach helped them load the tanks into Nancy's car after giving them directions. Then he gave a quick wave and headed back to the boat.

They soon arrived at the other store, and Ned climbed out and went around to open the trunk. He was reaching for the first tank when Nancy saw his face contort with pain. He cried out, jerking his hand away.

"What is it, Ned?"

"I think I just got bitten by something," Ned

said. He held up his hand, which had an ugly red mark on it.

Nancy peered into the trunk and saw a large insect crawling on one of the tanks. She leaned down to get a closer look—and her heart beat double time. Ned had just been bitten by a scorpion!

Chapter

Ten

WE HAVE to get you to the hospital right away, Ned," Nancy said in a worried voice. She knew that some scorpion bites were extremely dangerous.

"I'm okay, Nancy—really," Ned said, and climbed into the car next to her. "It just stings a little where the actual bite is."

Ned's hand was already swelling, Nancy could see. She drove as quickly as safety allowed, following a series of blue signs that pointed the way to Key West Hospital.

"I know you'll be fine, Ned," Nancy said reassuringly. She didn't want him to know how worried she really was. Glancing at him, Nancy could see that the swelling had already doubled in the short time they'd been driving.

"Hang on, Ned," she said, deftly maneuvering around some bicycles. "We're almost there."

It seemed an eternity before they spotted the red and white sign of the hospital's emergency room. Nancy pulled into a parking space next to an ambulance. She got out and hurried around to open the passenger door for Ned.

"Do you think you can walk, or should I get a wheelchair?" Nancy asked Ned. He looked as if he was beginning to get dizzy.

"I can walk—just don't ask me to do the high jump," Ned joked weakly as he climbed out of the car.

Inside the hospital they were quickly admitted to see an emergency room doctor. The doctor, who had short dark hair and a no-nonsense manner, was briskly reassuring as she examined the bite on Ned's hand.

"Don't worry, Ms. Drew," the doctor said to Nancy as she gave Ned a shot, "you'll have your boyfriend around for many years to come."

"Then the bite's not serious?" Nancy asked, holding her breath.

"A scorpion bite *can* be serious, but only to people who are severely allergic to insect venom, such as bee stings," the doctor explained. "In general, scorpions and other bugs like tarantulas are fairly harmless. They've just gotten a bad rap from all those horror movies. We'll keep you here a little while for observation, then send you home," she said to Ned.

Nancy felt a warm rush wash through her body. "I'm so relieved," she whispered, squeezing Ned's good hand.

"*You're* relieved?" Ned grinned. "I feel like a death sentence has just been lifted!"

About an hour later Nancy and Ned walked out of the emergency room.

"I'll call Sean again and tell him to go on without us—I want to take care of you back at the inn," Nancy said.

"No way!" Ned protested. "You heard the doctor say I'm fine. I'll just want to sleep anyway."

"If you're really sure . . ." Nancy said.

"Positive." Ned leaned over and kissed her on the cheek.

As they made their way back to the inn, Ned glanced at Nancy. "You've got that look, Nan, like you're figuring something out," he said after a while. "What wheels are turning behind those beautiful blue eyes?"

"I'm just wondering how that scorpion got into the trunk," Nancy replied. "It doesn't seem a likely place for an insect to hang out."

"Maybe it hitched a ride on something," Ned said. "Like one of the scuba tanks."

"Or was *given* a ride," Nancy said thoughtfully. "Could this have been Leif Dorning's way of sending a message from the *Sea Scorpion?*"

"Possibly. Only how did he know we'd be going into the trunk?" Ned asked her.

Nancy's eyes narrowed thoughtfully. "You're right, Ned. Only Zach knew that we'd be opening the trunk. In fact, he even helped us load those air tanks." She sighed. "If I know Zach, he'll swear that you're another victim of the curse of the *Ninfa Marina.*"

"Oh, yeah, the curse," Ned said, raising one dubious eyebrow.

"Either he really believes in it—or he wants *us* to," Nancy said. "I have to find out which."

Nancy pulled up in front of the Sunset Cove Inn to drop Ned off. "Get lots of sleep today," she told him. "I'll come back to check on you as soon as I get off the boat this afternoon." She gave him a quick hug.

"I want more than a hug," Ned whispered huskily. He tilted her chin toward him with his finger. Then he kissed her long and hard, until she felt a tingling warmth reach all the way down to her toes. "To be continued tonight," he said, opening the car door.

"Wow," Nancy said, still feeling the lingering effect of Ned's kiss. She couldn't wait until later!

Nancy stopped to have the tanks filled at Diver Dan's and then returned to the *Lady Jane*. Bess, George, and the others greeted her with anxious questions. All they knew was what Sean had told them after Nancy called from the emergency room a couple hours earlier.

"Sorry to hear about your friend," Zach muttered.

After Nancy reassured everyone that Ned would recover, they prepared to cast off.

"We're going back to the spot where we found the *Ninfa Marina*'s anchor," Sean told her. "It'll be a short day because of our delay, but I want to scour that area before dark. Another day when we have more time, I'll bring up the anchor itself."

By eleven o'clock the *Lady Jane* was pounding through choppy seas about a mile off Key West. Nancy, Bess, and George were standing outside on the deck in front of the pilothouse. Through its window, Nancy could see Zach guiding the boat. Sean and Talia were behind him, monitoring some equipment.

A big wave slapped against the boat's hull.

"Wow, it's getting rough," Bess said, clutching the rail for support.

"It sure is. Just look at those dark gray clouds on the horizon," George observed.

Nancy nodded. "It looks like there's a storm heading our way," she said, opening the door to the pilothouse.

"Hi, Nancy," Sean greeted her. "We've got something new on the subbottom profiler. Since this is close to the spot where we found the anchor, I think we should check it out." Zach cut the engine. "Talia, why don't you take a quick look around in the submersible," Sean continued. "But let's hurry. We may have a squall kicking up to the east."

Sean seemed to have accepted Talia's explanation for her involvement with Leif Dorning, Nancy noted. Nancy herself hadn't made up her mind about the marine archaeologist.

"Come on, Nancy," Talia said, tapping her on the shoulder. "Let's take the submersible down and have a look around."

Talia, Nancy, Zach, and Sean stepped out on the deck, joining Bess and George. Nancy checked out the tubular, metallic craft. The submersible had a robotic arm attached to one side, complete with a clawlike hand.

"We use that claw for heavy lifting underwater," Talia explained.

Bess stared apprehensively at the sub. "I can't believe you're actually going underwater in that tiny thing," she whispered to Nancy.

Talia and Zach used a small hydraulic lift to maneuver the submersible into the water. Then Nancy and Talia climbed over the rail and down a ladder to the water. The tiny sub was pitching wildly in the swells.

"Be careful, you two," George called from the deck above them.

Talia climbed through the hatch on top of the

sub, followed by Nancy. Talia shut the hatch, flipped a switch, and the submersible plunged under the roiling waves.

As soon as they were below the surface, Nancy felt they had entered another world. Except for the high-pitched drone of the submersible's small propellers, all was silent. A school of brilliantly colored fish swam before the window. By pushing something that resembled a gear stick, Talia nudged the submersible into still deeper water.

"It feels just like flying underwater," Nancy noted. She heard a crackling noise and then a voice came over the intercom.

"You there, guys?" It was Sean.

Talia picked up a small black microphone. "Even under water, we can communicate by radio," she explained to Nancy. "Right here, Sean," she spoke into the mike.

"You'd better hurry. It's getting kind of rough up here," Sean said. "See you topside soon."

As the craft nosed into still deeper water, Nancy glanced sideways at Talia. She really liked the marine archaeologist and had to remind herself that Talia was a major suspect.

"Were you aware that Leif Dorning's boat had been sabotaged, as well as Sean's?" she asked Talia.

Talia nodded. "I just hope he realizes that Sean had nothing to do with it," she said. "I hate to see the two of them fighting."

"And what about your feelings about Sean?" Nancy pressed, remembering the bitter letter that Talia had started writing. "Do you blame him for your brother's death?"

Talia sighed. "No, I don't really blame Sean for Jaime's death. It was just an accident. A senseless accident." Almost despite herself, Nancy had the gut feeling that Talia was telling the truth.

The sub was nearing the ocean floor. The water was very murky because of the weather on the surface. Talia shone the submersible's light on a large object in front of them. "Uh-oh. Looks like our treasure is just a pile of rocks," Talia said in disappointment. "I'll have to tell Sean we struck out."

"Zach seems to be convinced that all the trouble you've had has been caused by that curse," Nancy said as they headed back to the surface.

"Oh, that again," Talia said, rolling her eyes. "He's been going on about that dumb curse for at least six months. I got riled at him the other day because he tried to pin my brother's death on it. I think it was some wild idea that Hank Morley put in his head. He's pretty superstitious."

"Hank Morley?" Nancy echoed. "Are he and Zach friendly?"

"Oh, yes, very friendly," Talia replied. "Don't tell Sean, but I think Zach moonlights as a diver for Morley on the weekends."

"I didn't know that Morley was an active treasure hunter—"

Nancy broke off as Sean's voice came crackling over the radio. The signal sounded very weak.

"You two better come back to the surface right away," he said, urgently.

"What's up, Sean?" Talia spoke into the microphone.

A burst of static came over the speaker. There was a garbled transmission, and then Nancy thought she could make out the words *bad storm*.

"I'm not sure what he said, but it sounds serious," Talia said.

There was another burst of static, and then Nancy distinctly heard the word *sinking*.

"I don't know what you made of that," Nancy said to Talia, "but it sounded to me as though Sean just said the *Lady Jane* is sinking!"

Chapter

Eleven

COULD THE *Lady Jane* actually be sinking? It seemed impossible to Nancy.

"We have to get back to the surface as quickly as possible," Talia said. She pointed to an emergency toggle switch on the sub's control panel. "We can blow out the air tanks, which will shoot us to the surface like a rocket," she said. "But it can make for a pretty scary ride."

"Let's do it," Nancy agreed quickly, checking her seat belt.

Talia flipped the emergency switch. They heard a loud whooshing from the back of the sub. Then it started spinning and rising like a bubble.

Moments later the sub broke through to the surface. Huge ocean swells immediately picked up the tiny craft and tossed it around like a piece of driftwood. Angry black clouds overhead spattered sheets of rain onto the sub's view window.

Catching an occasional glimpse of the *Lady Jane,* Nancy could just make out Sean, George, and Bess standing at the rail. The *Lady Jane* appeared to be weathering the storm much better than they were.

"The *Lady Jane* looks okay." Nancy breathed a sigh of relief. "We must have got Sean's message wrong."

"Thank goodness," Talia replied. "It's going to be hard to get back on the boat in this weather," she added in a worried voice. She explained the docking procedure to Nancy. "Zach will maneuver the boat as close to us as possible while Sean tosses us a rope." Talia said, pulling back the bolts that fastened the sub's entry hatch. *"Catching* the rope is the tricky part."

When the ship got close to the drifting sub, Talia lifted the hatch and got drenched almost instantly. Sean tossed a line toward her, and after several tries, Talia caught it and fastened it to a hook on the side of the sub. Sean reeled them in using a portable winch, and then he and Talia labored together in the downpour to tether the sub to the side of the ship.

"What's going on?" Nancy asked Sean as soon as they were back on board in dry clothes. "We heard you say something about a boat sinking. Is there a problem with the *Lady Jane?"*

"No, it's the *Sea Scorpion* that's in trouble. We just received a distress signal from Leif Dorning," Sean said breathlessly.

"Oh, no!" Talia gasped, and stopped toweling her hair dry for a minute.

"We have to try to locate him," Sean said.

They went to the pilothouse, where Zach was bent over the radio. The rain was a mere mist now and the ocean swells had flattened out a little. The *Lady Jane* was riding almost smoothly in the still, gloomy darkness.

"I've got the *Sea Scorpion's* coordinates," he said. "The Coast Guard is on the way, but we're less than a mile away, so I think we can reach her first."

"What happened?" Nancy asked.

"All we know is that the *Sea Scorpion* is taking on water. We got a distress call about twenty minutes ago," Zach replied.

Sean threw the engine into gear, and the *Lady Jane* surged forward. Meanwhile, Zach radioed Dorning to say that the *Lady Jane* was on its way.

Nancy, George, and Talia went out on deck to scan the horizon for a glimpse of the black-hulled boat.

"There it is!" Talia cried out after about ten minutes.

As they drew alongside the *Sea Scorpion,* Nancy could tell it was in serious trouble. The vessel had already taken on a lot of water—its stern was sinking fast. Already the top deck was more than a foot underwater. Nancy could see Leif and his crew of three men loading equipment onto a motorized dinghy.

"We have to concentrate on getting everyone off safely," Sean said. "Then we'll unload as much equipment as possible." It was a long, dangerous process because the wind had kicked up and the sea was rough again with giant waves breaking over both boats. The two crews used the dinghy to ferry equipment onto the *Lady Jane.*

Dorning was the last person to leave the sinking vessel. Once on board the *Lady Jane* he hugged Talia as he focused on his ship with an agonized expression.

"I can't understand what happened," he said. "One minute everything was fine—the next minute we were swamped."

Before long a Coast Guard rescue helicopter came into view and hovered above them. Since everyone had gotten off the *Sea Scorpion* safely, there was little for it to do.

It was nearing the end for Leif's boat. Nancy and the others watched silently as it slipped away. Its graceful bow rose high in the air, then began its slow slide into its final descent. The *Sea Scorpion* vanished forever.

After a moment of silence Sean walked up to Dorning.

"I know how you must feel, Dorning," he said with a catch in his voice. "I'm sorry it happened."

"Are you?" Dorning asked with a trace of hostility. "I owe you one for rescuing my crew, Sean. But I haven't forgotten your little raid on my ship the other night."

"Did you notice anything unusual today before you started taking on water?" Nancy asked Dorning, ignoring his criticism of her.

Dorning glared for a moment without answering, then he sighed and answered. "Not really. This morning we were all so excited—one of my crew members had found a gold doubloon. We thought it might be from the *Ninfa Marina*."

"You found a gold piece from the *Ninfa Marina* this morning?" Sean echoed excitedly.

Dorning nodded. "After we found it we went back in to refuel at Hank Morley's and have an early lunch. After lunch we went back out, and that's when all the trouble started."

"So you left the ship unattended at Hank's shop for a while," Nancy said thoughtfully.

"Well, Hank kept an eye on it." Dorning shrugged. "I still don't understand what happened. There was a cracking sound, and then the bilge pump wouldn't work. Water just kept rising in the hold. We couldn't even find the leak."

"Do you think the leak could have been the result of sabotage?" Nancy asked.

Dorning shrugged. "Maybe," he said in an exasperated tone.

One of Dorning's crew had been standing and listening with his eyes wide and staring. "It must have been the curse," the burly sailor said in frightened hushed tones. "The curse of the *Ninfa Marina!*"

"Keep a lid on it, Murphy," Dorning snapped. "You know I don't have any patience for that kind of talk."

Nancy saw Zach approach the man, and the two men began an intense conversation about the curse of the *Ninfa Marina.*

Nancy turned away and walked by herself. She wanted a moment alone to think things through. She was recalling that Talia had said that Zach and Hank Morley were close friends, and now it appeared that Morley had access to the *Sea Scorpion* just before it sank.

George and Bess came up and joined her. "What do you think all this means, Nancy?" George asked.

Nancy looked over her shoulder to make sure no one could overhear. "Until yesterday, Dorning was high on my list of suspects. Now it seems that he's been the victim of sabotage—just like Sean."

"Where does that leave us?" Bess asked.

"The only person I *know* is involved in all this is that bearded guy—the one who left me the skull and the warning note," she said. "And so far, all my information about *him* has come from one source—Hank Morley."

George's brown eyes lit up with understanding. "And Dorning has just told us that Hank Morley was alone with the *Sea Scorpion* before she sank today."

Nancy nodded. "Exactly. The question is, how does Hank Morley tie into Rusty's murder? I think it's time I did a little checking on our friend Mr. Morley."

When they arrived back at the marina, Sean and Dorning's crews began unloading the equipment that had been salvaged from Dorning's ship. "This'll keep us busy for a few hours," Sean said to Nancy.

"We'll head back to the inn and pick up Ned," she replied. Nancy, Bess, and George drove directly to the Sunset Cove Inn to find Ned waiting on the front porch.

"Hi, Bess. Hi, George. Hi, Nan," Ned said, greeting Nancy with a kiss. "I feel great now. See?" He held his hand up to show them all that the swelling from the scorpion bite had disappeared.

Bess and George excused themselves to change for dinner.

"Are you sure you're okay?" Nancy asked softly after the girls had gone.

Ned picked her up in a bear hug and swung her

around. "Does that answer your question?" he said lightly.

"Enough! I believe you!" Nancy protested laughingly. "And after I rest and get changed for dinner, I'll even put you to the test."

"A romantic test, I hope?" Ned asked teasingly.

She grinned. "That, too—but right now I'm talking about my case."

Ned turned serious. "What happened today?" he asked.

Nancy filled him in on the developments of the day, including the sinking of the *Sea Scorpion*. "I have a hunch that was no accident," she asserted. "I may need your help to do a little snooping around Hank Morley's shop."

"Consider it done," Ned replied.

Nancy smiled. "Thanks," she said. "But first, I think we're entitled to eat some dinner, don't you?" Ned nodded vigorously. *"After* I shower and change," she added.

"I'm too stuffed to do any spying tonight," Bess said a couple of hours later, pushing back from the table. She, Nancy, Ned, and George had just polished off a huge crock of spicy chili and corn muffins, with pitchers of iced tea, at Mile Marker 4, a tiny roadside café along Highway 1.

"That's all right, Bess," Nancy said. "You can wait for us in the car at Hank's place. We'll need a lookout, anyway." Nancy had asked Bess and George to join them spying that night.

A kindly-looking woman with short gray hair suddenly appeared beside Bess's chair. Nancy recognized her as the hostess who had seated them. "Does anyone here drive a white convertible?" the woman asked.

"I do," Nancy replied.

The woman held out a folded square of paper. "Someone left a note that your lights are on," she said.

"Thanks," Nancy said, pocketing the note. "I can't believe I did such a dumb thing," she said lightly. "I hope the car battery hasn't run down."

"What a pain," Bess sympathized. "I know because I leave my lights on at least once a month."

"I'll be right back, guys," Nancy said, rising and making her way through the front door to the restaurant parking lot. She glanced at her car and was puzzled to note that the lights were *not* on.

Whoever left the note must have been mistaken, Nancy thought. She shrugged and started back toward the front door. Then, on second thought, she reached into her pocket and pulled out the note the hostess had given her.

Nancy drew in a sharp breath. The heavy scrawl on the note—it was the same handwriting that had been on the threatening note she'd received the day before. It was the bearded guy again! Nancy realized with a jolt. He must have lied about the headlights to lure her outside.

Just then she heard a rustling noise off to her left. Instinctively, she ducked and dove behind a car, but it was too late.

Nancy saw the flash of a gun at the same moment she heard a muffled shot ring out. A split second later she felt a searing pain in her left arm. Oh, no, she thought. I've been hit!

Chapter

Twelve

NANCY WINCED and grabbed her left arm. Gritting her teeth, she made herself check the wound. Then she let out her breath on a rush of relief.

The bullet had grazed her upper arm. Despite the burning sensation, Nancy could tell it wasn't really serious.

Ned and George came bursting through the restaurant door, followed by Bess.

"Nancy! Are you all right?" Ned cried out, kneeling beside her. "You've been hurt."

"A bullet just grazed my arm. I'll be okay," Nancy assured him.

"I'll go get some towels to use as a compress," Bess said. She hurried back into the restaurant.

George bent over Nancy anxiously. "Did you

111

see who fired at you?" she asked. "Was it the bearded guy?"

Nancy nodded. "I didn't see him. But I just realized that the handwriting on this note the hostess gave me matches the writing on the note in the skull. So I'm sure it had to be the bearded guy. It looks like this time he meant business."

By now some of the restaurant staff and other guests had gathered in an anxious circle around Nancy. Bess pushed through them as she returned with the towels.

"We'll use these to stop the bleeding," she said, pressing a towel gently against Nancy's arm. "Someone inside already called the police and an ambulance."

"I don't need an ambulance," Nancy protested, but Ned shook his head.

"That arm needs to be looked at right away," he said firmly. "Nan, when I think of what might have happened . . ." Ned choked up and was unable to finish his sentence.

Within minutes the police and ambulance arrived. As the paramedic bandaged her arm, Nancy described the attack to a detective. She mentioned the case she was working on, including a description of the bearded guy. Nancy and the detective talked with the restaurant hostess. The hostess confirmed that the man who left the note about Nancy's car lights being on had had a beard.

The detective dispatched a description of the man and his gray sedan. If spotted, he should be stopped for questioning in connection with the shooting.

An officer found the bullet that had grazed Nancy embedded in a tree. He dug the slug out and dropped it into a plastic evidence bag.

"I'll make a note on my police report about a possible tie-in to Sean Mahoney's case," the detective said to Nancy. "That's about all I can do at this point."

The paramedic finished bandaging Nancy's arm, then handed her a prescription for antibiotics. "There's a risk of infection, even with a minor gunshot wound," he explained. "You'll need to take it easy for the next twenty-four hours."

After the police and paramedics left, Nancy returned to the car with Ned, George, and Bess.

"I still want to check out Hank Morley's place tonight," she said to her friends. "Somehow I feel he's the key to everything that's been happening."

"No way," George and Ned said in unison.

"You heard what the paramedic said, Nancy," Bess said. "Your health could be at stake."

"That's right," Ned insisted. "We're going to pick up this medication and head straight back to the hotel."

Nancy could see there was no use arguing with

them. "All right, you win," she said. "But just for tonight."

Nancy was out of bed before anyone else the next morning. Her left arm ached underneath the bandage, but she forced herself to ignore it and pulled on a long-sleeved T-shirt to hide the bandage.

By eight o'clock, Nancy, Ned, George, and Bess were on board the *Lady Jane*. Sean was visibly upset about the attack on Nancy the night before.

"The police called me last night," he said. "I don't want you to take any more chances, Nancy," he said anxiously. "I'd feel awful if anything else happened to you."

Nancy brushed off Sean's concern. "Last night's attack tells me that the bearded man and his accomplice know we're closing in on them," she told Sean. "We can't afford to back off now."

While the crew got the *Lady Jane* ready to go, and George, Ned, and Bess made a run to the doughnut shop, Nancy went off to survey Hank Morley's shop and was disappointed to find him already at work. There would be no chance to nose around until that night.

When Nancy got back to the ship, Zach was just heading for the pilothouse to start the engine and cast off. Nancy looked around. Everyone seemed to be in a lighter mood, maybe because the sun was out.

Talia was demonstrating to Bess how the submersible worked. Next to them, George and Sean had their heads bent together, whispering. Nancy saw George peer up into Sean's eyes and smile.

"How are you feeling, Nancy?" Ned handed her a cool drink that he had just brought up from the galley.

"Good, thanks," Nancy replied, taking a sip of the lemonade and sitting in a deck chair. She was watching Talia with a troubled expression.

Ned followed her glance. "Something's bothering you," Ned said in a quiet voice. "What is it?"

"I still haven't figured out who's working with the bearded man—Talia, Zach, or Hank Morley," Nancy said. "I know that guy wrote the note that lured Sean to the scene of Rusty's murder, and he's probably tied in to the sabotage, too. That makes me positive he's working with someone on the inside. And the fact that Dorning's ship went down yesterday makes me worry that we're running out of time."

"I know you'll figure it out," Ned said. He leaned over and gently stroked her cheek.

"Thanks, Ned," she said gratefully.

Nancy rose from her chair. "I'm going to find Zach," she said to Ned. "I never had a chance to talk to him about the scorpion incident the other day. I want to make sure he didn't have a hand in it."

Nancy went to the door of the pilothouse and opened it to find Zach using the ship-to-shore radio. He appeared startled to see Nancy and stopped talking abruptly. He hung up the radio mike.

"I was just getting a weather report," Zach said quickly. "Do you need something, Nancy?"

"I wanted to ask you about that scorpion we found in my trunk the other day," Nancy said. "Does that sort of thing happen often around here?"

Zach nodded. "Scorpions are kind of shy little creatures. That's why you usually find them in dark, out-of-the way places, like closets."

"I think someone may have put that scorpion in my trunk deliberately," Nancy said slowly.

"Then I'd say you've jumped to conclusions," Zach said, his eyes flashing. "And if you're thinking that *I* had anything to do with it, you're dead wrong."

Just then Sean entered the pilothouse, interrupting their conversation. "I want to take another look at the *Ninfa Marina's* anchor on the scanner," he said to Zach. "We'll fan out from this spot in concentric circles to search for the treasure."

As she listened to them talking, Nancy considered Zach's reaction to her questions about the scorpion attack. She had barely pressed him about it when he had turned angry. That was the reaction of someone with something to hide, she thought to herself.

Sean was bent over the subbottom profiler. "I see something kind of unusual right down below us," he said. "Look at this, guys."

Nancy and Zach checked the scanner. The screen was showing the outline of a series of some vaguely squarelike shapes on the ocean floor.

"I've never seen anything quite like that before," Sean said slowly, "but I think it's definitely worth checking out."

Bess wasn't certified for scuba diving, and they had no wet suit for Ned, so those two had to stay on the boat with Zach while Nancy, George, Sean, and Talia dove.

"Should you be diving with that arm injury, Nancy?" Sean said doubtfully.

"It's nothing more than a scrape now, Sean," Nancy assured him.

Sean looked worried. "All right, but I'm going to keep a careful eye on you," he said, picking up a black specimen bag. "I don't want to lose anyone else to the treasure of the *Ninfa Marina.*"

Talia picked up a gadget that looked like a saucer stuck on the end of a stick. "This is an underwater metal detector," she explained. "Over the years, things get so encrusted that it's hard to know what you're looking at. This tells us what's metal and what isn't."

The four divers double-checked their scuba gear. One by one, they plunged into the ocean.

As Nancy descended she found that she was happy to be in the water even though her arm ached a little.

She, George, and Talia followed Sean down toward a cluster of strange-looking mounds. At first the whitish formations looked like coral.

Nancy was struck by the beauty of the undersea scene. Delicate, transparent jellyfish hovered above the white mounds like sea ghosts, Nancy thought.

Sean increased his speed as he approached the mounds. Excitedly he motioned to Talia, and she nodded and swam over to him. Nancy watched as she clicked on the metal detector and passed it over one of the mounds. The metal detector emitted a loud screeching sound that made everyone jump.

Following Sean's lead, Nancy started scraping back the surface of one of the white mounds. Then she gasped. Her scraping had revealed the unmistakable glitter of gold.

Nancy soon realized that the mounds were actually stacks and stacks of gold and silver bars!

Talia reached down and picked up one of the silver bars—it was as big as a loaf of bread.

Nancy exchanged an excited look with George.

All around them were at least fifty mounds like the one they'd just found—each one probably containing heaps of gold and silver bars.

The discovery was staggering. Spread out on the sand was the long-lost treasure of the *Ninfa Marina!*

Chapter
Thirteen

Nancy felt totally overwhelmed. The gold had to be worth millions of dollars.

Sean and Talia hugged each other joyfully. There could be no doubt—the treasure of the *Ninfa Marina* had been found!

Nancy felt a tingling rush as she took in the treasure lying before them. She reached down and picked up one of the golden bars. It was as long as her hand, and it felt smooth and heavy.

Sean opened the specimen bag and loaded two gold bars into it. Then he signaled for everyone to return to the surface.

As soon as Sean broke the surface, he yanked the regulator out of his mouth. Then he reached into his bag, pulled out a gold bar, and held it up.

"We found it!" he shouted to Zach, Ned, and

Bess, who were watching from the deck. "We found the treasure! It's right underneath us."

"I don't believe it!" Bess exclaimed.

Nancy, George, and Talia surfaced behind Sean, each carrying another gold bar. "I'm so happy for you, Sean," George said excitedly. He grabbed George and happily hugged her in the water.

Zach's jaw was hanging open. He reached over the side of the boat and took the bar that Sean held in his outstretched hand. Then he sank weakly into a deck chair, staring at the bar.

"I've been looking forward to this day for more than a year!" Sean crowed happily as he, Talia, Nancy, and George climbed from the water and slipped off their wet suits.

Then everyone was hugging everyone. They all seemed awestruck by the discovery.

As the celebrating continued, Nancy approached Sean and drew him aside. "I hate to be a wet blanket, Sean, but I think we should take some precautions right away."

"Um—what precautions?" Sean responded in a slightly dazed manner. Nancy could see that he was having trouble focusing on anything other than the treasure.

"We need to make sure that no one outside this ship finds out about the treasure tonight," Nancy said. "You could be in danger."

121

Sean paused and took a deep breath. "You're probably right," he agreed. "I got so caught up in the moment, I forgot that someone may be plotting to get his hands on it. I'll go down and put salvage flags around the treasure. That's the first step in making an official claim. I'll call Karen, my lawyer, tomorrow and have her file a claim with the state. In the meantime, I'd like to anchor here overnight. I want to bring up as much treasure as possible over the next day or so."

"That sounds good," Nancy replied. Then she remembered Zach's interrupted conversation on the ship's radio. "I know this sounds drastic, but I think we should disable the radio for tonight," she said. "That way, nobody can relay our position to anyone off the boat."

"All right," Sean said. "I'll take care of that myself. Anything else?"

Nancy shook her head and checked to make sure no one was listening. "Just keep your eyes open tonight for any unusual behavior. If either Zach or Talia is going to make a move, they'll do it now that the treasure's been found."

"I'll go remove the radio fuse." Sean nodded and then headed for the pilothouse.

Nancy and Ned strolled toward the bow, talking about the treasure. Nancy watched as Talia loaded a vat of liquid plastic into the submersible.

"We use this goop to coat some of the more delicate things we'll bring up from below," she explained. "It helps us keep the pieces as intact as possible."

"Nancy, Ned—can we talk to you for a second?" Nancy saw George and Bess standing at her side.

"Sure, let's go below," Nancy replied. They went downstairs through the galley and into a tiny bunk room. Nancy shut the door.

"What's on your mind?" she asked her friends.

George spoke first. "We saw you talking with Sean and figured you must be thinking about what's going to happen next. We wanted to know if we could help."

"Thanks, guys," Nancy felt a warm rush of affection for her friends. "Actually, I'll need help staking out the pilothouse tonight. I have a feeling that either Zach or Talia will try to radio the news of the treasure to someone on shore—maybe the bearded guy."

"All right," George said. "We can take turns guarding the radio."

"Great." Nancy smiled.

For the rest of the afternoon the crew of the *Lady Jane* worked to secure the treasure. Zach set out a floating ring of red-and-green salvage flags. Talia made several dives to the bottom with the submersible to help Sean photograph and tally the treasure mounds.

By supper time everyone was exhausted from both the excitement and hard work. As soon as the sun sank below the horizon, Bess and George set out a meal they'd made from what was left in the galley.

"Sailor's stew!" Sean exclaimed happily. "Thanks!" He smiled at George.

"Bess gets most of the credit," George said, blushing. "But I did chop the vegetables."

After dinner Nancy found Ned staking out the radio in the pilothouse. "Have you seen anyone yet?" she asked him.

Ned nodded. "Talia came by a little while ago," Ned said. "She looked surprised to see me sitting in here. She said she wanted to check a chart in here. Zach came in at one point, too. He said he needed to check some instruments."

Too bad there was no way to know which of them might have been planning to use the radio, Nancy thought.

Next it was Nancy's turn to keep watch. By then it was almost ten o'clock. The ship was quiet as everyone retired to his or her bunk.

Bess and George appeared at the door to the pilothouse. "Sean fixed up spare bunks for us," Bess said to Nancy, stifling a yawn. "We'd like to turn in."

Ned, who was sitting next to Nancy in the pilothouse, stretched and rubbed his eyes. "I guess we're all pretty wiped out by all the excitement today," he said.

"Get some sleep, Ned," Nancy said to him. "I'll stay on the stakeout."

"Thanks." He leaned over and kissed her gently. "Call me when it's my turn to stand watch," he said, and headed out the door.

Nancy made herself as comfortable as possible on the chair in the pilothouse. Her mind was focused on the treasure and their situation on board the *Lady Jane*. It's possible I was wrong in thinking that the bearded man was working with someone on board, Nancy reminded herself. Perhaps Rusty was his only accomplice. The bearded man could have killed Rusty over the gold ingot. But somehow Nancy was certain that someone else was involved.

She could feel how tired she was all the way down to her bones. It was quiet except for the sound of waves lapping gently against the side of the boat. Despite her best efforts to stay awake, she finally fell into a deep but fitful sleep.

Nancy awoke with a vague feeling that something was wrong. She pressed a tiny light on her wristwatch. It was 5:30 A.M.

Getting up, she wandered out on deck. It was pitch-black, and she couldn't see a thing.

"Ouch!" Nancy muttered as she stumbled over

something on the deck. She looked down and recognized the *Lady Jane*'s anchor line. "Wait a second, what's this?" Bending forward, Nancy saw that the metal links of the anchor line had been cut with a pair of metal clippers that were lying nearby. The boat must be adrift! she realized with a jolt.

Alarm spread through her as she felt her way along the railing toward the bow. She searched the darkness, at last making out the outline of some black shapes looming in front of the boat.

Nancy's heart leapt. The *Lady Jane* had drifted almost all the way back to shore. The boat was about to crash into some huge rocks!

Chapter

Fourteen

NANCY COULD SEE the jagged boulders just a few yards ahead of the *Lady Jane*. Quick as a flash, she raced back to the pilothouse.

She winced as she stumbled over something in the darkness and felt a twinge in her arm under her bandage. Picking herself up, she groped along the wall until she found the door to the pilothouse.

The instrument panel gave off just enough of a glow for Nancy to see the control switches. She spotted a red alarm button and pressed it. A high-pitched siren began to sound throughout the ship.

Please let me be able to get the engine started before we hit those rocks, Nancy thought. Adrenaline pumped through her as she twisted the ignition key, just as she had seen Zach and Sean do. To her relief, the engine sputtered, then roared to life. Nancy grabbed the steering wheel and threw the throttle into full reverse, bracing herself for the sudden lurch of the boat. The helm responded quickly, allowing her to back the boat away from the rocks.

Then Sean burst into the pilothouse, with Ned close on his heels.

"What's the problem?" Sean demanded. "Why are we moving?"

"The anchor line's been cut," Nancy explained. "I'd say we've been drifting for quite a while. We narrowly missed hitting those rocks over there." She pointed through the window toward the shore, which was lit by the first streaks of dawn. Sean's and Ned's faces blanched when they saw how narrow their escape had been.

Turning the helm over to Sean, Nancy went outside with Ned to look around. Bess, George, and Talia were huddled together, talking in anxious tones.

Nancy checked to account for everyone on board. "Where's Zach?" Nancy asked Talia.

"I'll look for him," George said, heading for the bow.

"Maybe he slept through the alarm," Bess suggested. "I'll go below and look for him, too," she said.

Following George toward the bow with Ned, Nancy suddenly realized that the *Lady Jane*'s small, motorized dinghy was missing from its berth near the front deck.

"Look, guys! The dinghy's gone—and I bet Zach's stolen it!" Nancy gasped.

"Gone?" Ned echoed. "Where could he go in the middle of the night?"

"I wouldn't be surprised if he left to contact the bearded guy," Nancy said grimly. "They must be working together."

Bess returned from inside the ship. "Zach's locker is cleaned out," she said, "but I found these on the floor of the galley." She held out a pile of papers and photos. "He must have dropped this stuff on his way out."

"Let me see it, Bess." Nancy took the pile of papers and sifted through them. A photo dropped to the floor.

Nancy picked it up and peered at it. It was a picture of Zach standing next to Hank Morley and another, younger man.

"The man in this picture looks familiar to me," Nancy said, staring at the tall, thin, brown-haired man next to Hank. Then she snapped her fingers. "He's clean-shaven in this photo, but that's definitely the bearded man!"

Nancy headed to the pilothouse, followed by Ned, Bess, and George. Sean was at the helm. She showed him the photo. "Do you recognize the guy in the picture standing next to Hank Morley and Zach?" she asked him. "He's the guy who took a shot at me yesterday."

Sean peered at the photo. "That's Hank Morley's son, Marcus," he said, handing the photo back to Nancy. "I haven't seen him around for a long time. He never had a beard, so I didn't connect him with your description."

Nancy took in a sharp breath. "Then Hank's son probably killed Rusty, as well. It was his handwriting on the note that set you up for Rusty's murder."

"I can't believe Hank's son and Zach have it in for me!" Sean shook his head. "Do you think Hank is involved in this scheme, too?" he asked her.

Nancy nodded. "I remember the day I chased Hank's son—Marcus—into Hank's shop. Hank totally covered for him. I think that proves Hank is working with them. I'll bet anything Zach took the dinghy in order to contact the Morleys about the treasure."

"Then we have to get back to the treasure before they do," Sean said anxiously.

Nancy nodded. "Definitely."

Talia came into the pilothouse. She looked shocked when Sean told her about Zach and the Morleys. "I always knew Zach and Morley were friends," she said. "But I can't believe he'd plot against you like that, Sean."

Using ocean charts, Talia laid out a return course to the treasure. It turned out they'd drifted about three miles from their original location.

Meanwhile, Nancy asked Sean to replace the radio fuse. "We may need to call the Coast Guard for help if we run into Zach and the Morleys," she explained. "But I hope that won't be necessary."

While the *Lady Jane* pounded through the waves back to the treasure, Nancy headed to the lounge cabin with George, Ned, and Bess.

"Do you really think Zach and the Morleys were behind Rusty Jones's murder, Nancy?" George asked.

Nancy nodded. "I still don't know exactly why Rusty was murdered, but there's no doubt in my mind that they were in on it," she said. "Between the three of them, they could have rigged all of the sabotage incidents. They must have gotten access to Leif Dorning's boat somehow, too. We know that Leif's boat sank after he stopped to refuel at Hank's yesterday. My guess is that Hank sabotaged his boat on other occasions, as well."

"I see." Ned's eyes lit up with understanding. "They rigged it so that Dorning blamed Sean for the incidents on his ship, just as Sean blamed Dorning for the sabotage on board the *Lady Jane*."

"And Zach tried to confuse everything by

talking about that ridiculous curse," Talia fumed.

The sky was beginning to brighten with the new day. Nancy, George, Bess, and Ned went to the bow to look for the floating ring of salvage flags that they'd set out the day before. No other boats were on the horizon.

George scanned the ocean with a pair of binoculars she'd borrowed from Sean. "There are the flags," she said excitedly.

Sean maneuvered the *Lady Jane* into position alongside them. "We don't have an anchor, so we'll have to use the engine to keep the ship in one spot," he called forward to Nancy. "Talia's going to take the helm while I go below to make sure the treasure is still okay."

Nancy, Ned, George, and Bess met up with Sean on the aft deck, where Sean was pulling on his wet suit. George helped him double-check his equipment before he fell into the sea. Nancy watched a pool of bubbles rise from the spot where he descended.

Nancy scanned the horizon. "Hey, there's a boat!" she said, pointing west. "Lend me the binoculars, George," she said. When George handed them over, Nancy raised the glasses to her eyes. She could make out an old wooden boat. Three men were standing on its deck.

Nancy felt her pulse quicken. "Oh, no, that's

Hank Morley's boat," she announced in a tight voice. "And he's got his son and Zach with him."

"Looks like we're in for a showdown," Ned said grimly, squinting to see the other boat.

"I'll say," Nancy said. She looked at the men again. "Ned, they're carrying guns."

"Guns!" Bess's face turned white. "What are we going to do?"

Nancy turned to Ned. "Ned, I want you to go to the pilothouse and tell Talia to radio the Coast Guard. Tell them it's an emergency!"

"Okay," Ned said.

Nancy watched nervously as Hank Morley pulled his boat within a few hundred feet of the *Lady Jane*. Then he stopped and dropped anchor.

"What are they doing?" George asked. Morley and his son were unhooking a small, cigar-shaped craft that was tethered to the side of the boat. Zach stood behind them, wearing a wet suit.

With a start, Nancy suddenly realized what the smaller craft was. "It's a submersible!" Nancy exclaimed, lowering the binoculars. "I saw it at Morley's shop the other day. So he was lying when he told me it belonged to one of his rich customers."

"They're going to try to grab the treasure," George said in a worried voice. "Nancy, Sean's down there alone. He could be in danger!"

"I know," Nancy said, frowning. "We have to help him."

Talia joined them. "Ned's got the helm," she said to Nancy. "He's trying to contact the Coast Guard, but so far we can't raise anyone. I came back here to see if I could help."

Nancy said, "Talia, you and I need to go below in the sub. Morley's about to go down in *his* sub, possibly to hurt Sean. We may have to scare Morley off."

"Okay," Talia said. She swiftly readied the submersible for launching. Bess and George helped them swing the sub out over the waves and lower it into the water. Then Talia and Nancy climbed over the side and into the sub.

"We don't have time to go through the safety checklist," Talia said as she sealed the hatch. "We'll just have to cross our fingers and hope that all systems are go."

"Consider them crossed," Nancy said grimly as the sub plunged under the waves.

Once they were underwater, Nancy peered through the view window for any glimpse of Sean or the treasure. All she could see was shimmering expanses of water.

Finally they neared the ocean floor. There at last was Sean, swimming just below them near one of the treasure mounds.

"Sean looks okay," Nancy said with a sigh of

relief. "I don't see Morley's sub anywhere around."

Just then a dark shadow moved across Sean. Her pulse quickening, Nancy spotted a diver closing in on him, clutching a lethal-looking fishing spear in his fist.

"Where did that guy come from?" Nancy exclaimed to Talia. "I thought Morley was in his submersible."

"That's Zach," Talia announced grimly. "I recognize that yellow stripe on his wet suit. He must have gone into the water while we were busy launching the sub."

Nancy could see that Zach was closing the distance between himself and Sean. He raised the spear to strike, its tip a foot from Sean's back.

Chapter

Fifteen

NANCY KNEW she had to do something to stop Zach, and fast!

"Talia, can you maneuver the sub so that we move right behind Zach?" Nancy asked. "Let's give that rat a taste of his own medicine."

"Great idea," Talia said, nosing the craft down. She pushed the throttle to maximum speed to overtake Zach.

Zach appeared to be startled as the sub appeared overhead. He dropped the spear and moved slowly toward the surface.

"Good work, Talia!" Nancy cried. Sean raised his head to them and waved. He was safe for the moment.

Suddenly Nancy saw Sean begin to point and wave more frantically. "It looks like he's trying to warn us about something," Nancy observed. "Talia, I think we'd better——"

Nancy was suddenly thrown back against her seat hard.

"What was that?" Nancy exclaimed. She turned in time to see Hank Morley bearing down on them in his own submersible!

"Morley just rammed us!" Talia said. She maneuvered around a rocky outcropping to escape Morley.

Nancy felt something cold and wet on her arm. Looking down she realized that a trickle of seawater was leaking into the tiny cabin.

"Talia, we've sprung a leak!" Nancy cried.

"Something ruptured during the collision," Talia said tensely. "We'll have to make an emergency ascent, otherwise we could drown."

Nancy shook her head. "We can't just abandon Sean. Hank Morley will kill him," she said. "We have to find a way to stop that leak."

More water was trickling in now—they didn't have much time. Nancy glanced around the inside of the sub. Her gaze fell on the vat of liquid plastic that Talia had placed in there the day before. "What about this?" she asked Talia, pointing to the vat.

"The polymer—great idea!" Talia exclaimed. "It should plug up the leak, like glue." She reached behind the seat to open the vat.

Nancy spotted Hank Morley's sub gliding silently around the rock pile. "Uh-oh. It looks like Morley's going to charge us again," Nancy said. "We've got to stall for time."

Just then her eye fell on the radio microphone, and she picked it up. "What radio channel would Morley use?" she asked Talia.

"Probably just the standard open channel," Talia replied. "Just key the mike and talk into it."

Nancy depressed the mike key. "Morley, are you there?" she spoke slowly. Through the window, she could only make out a shadowy outline of someone sitting inside the other sub.

There was a moment of silence. Then Morley's voice came over the speaker. "You might as well give up and go back to the surface, Nancy," Morley said. "The treasure's already mine."

"What makes you think you're going to get away with stealing it from Sean?" Nancy countered. "There are too many witnesses who'd testify that he found it first."

"Unfortunately for you, the *Lady Jane* is about to have a bad accident—and all hands on board will be lost," Morley said with a chilling laugh. "So much for witnesses."

Nancy felt cold sweat form on her brow. It was clear that Morley would stop at nothing to get his hands on the treasure. She glanced at Talia, who had just finished plastering the leak with the liquid plastic.

"We'll need a few minutes for it to dry," Talia whispered.

"I'm curious, Morley," Nancy spoke into the mike again. "What kind of accident are you talking about?"

"The kind that sends you all to the bottom of the sea," he growled. "Of course, everyone will blame your deaths on the curse of the *Ninfa Marina.*"

Suddenly all the strange incidents on board the *Lady Jane* made sense to Nancy. "Is that why you and Zach staged all those accidents on board Sean's and Dorning's boats? So that people would start believing in the curse?" she asked.

"That's right," Morley said smugly. "Zach did the sabotage on the *Lady Jane,* and my son and I rigged the accidents on Dorning's boat. We had to escalate things when you started nosing around," he continued. "Zach put the scorpion in your trunk, and Marcus followed you to the inn to plant the skull as a warning. Too bad you didn't get the message. You were lucky to escape when he took that shot at you outside the restaurant, but you won't get away this time."

Nancy tried to stifle a prickling sense of fear. "I'm sure you were responsible for the sinking of the *Sea Scorpion,*" she prodded.

"That was easy to set up," Morley boasted. "I disabled Dorning's pump system when they were refueling. Then I drilled a small hole in the outer hull. It was only a matter of time before she went down. I thought Dorning was about to discover the main treasure pile, so I wanted his ship out of the way—permanently."

"Very clever," Nancy said. "And you managed to set things up so that Sean and Dorning would accuse each other of sabotage."

"They were already so competitive, it was easy to play them against each other," Morley explained.

"And what about Rusty?" Nancy pressed. "You killed him, but why?"

"Unfortunately, Rusty discovered our scheme when he caught Zach setting the engine fire on the *Lady Jane,*" Morley said. "Zach scared him into staying quiet, but we knocked him off later, anyway. Marcus and I lured Rusty to the boat house on a ruse. After we killed him, Marcus tracked you down and left the phony note for Sean."

Nancy suddenly recalled how uneasy Rusty had been after the engine fire that first day on Sean's boat. Now she knew why—he was being threatened by Zach.

"And you set Sean up for Rusty's murder. That *was* clever," Nancy replied.

"Yes. Zach grabbed the ingot and we planted it at Rusty's to give Sean a motive for going after the old guy. We figured the police would suspect Sean right away, but Sean even helped us more by putting his fingerprints all over the murder weapon," he said, cackling.

"My plan all along was to let Dorning and Sean lead me to the gold," Morley continued. "Now all that's left is for me to arrange the final, fatal accident and claim the treasure for myself."

Nancy could see Morley's sub was moving closer. It was close enough now for her to see his cruel expression through the window.

"Let's get ready," Nancy whispered to Talia. "When the moment comes, we'll need to attack *him* before he attacks *us.*"

Talia nodded and swallowed nervously. She poised her hand over the throttle.

"Enough talk." Morley's voice was a harsh rasp over the radio speaker. "Time to die."

Nancy felt a surge of fear as Morley's sub lurched toward them. "Now, Talia!" she yelled.

Talia depressed the throttle so that they shot straight for Morley's sub. Then she veered slightly upward so that her sub's robotic arm smashed against Morley's view window like an iron fist.

The blow cracked Morley's view window in half. Through the glass they could see Morley frantically trying to stop seawater from leaking into his sub.

"We got him!" Talia cried happily as Morley pulled away and made an emergency ascent to the surface.

Nancy let out a huge breath of relief. Morley

was out of the way—for a moment, at least. "We'd better go after him," Nancy said. "But first I want to make sure that Sean is all right."

She spotted Sean swimming toward them around the rock pile. He was holding Zach's spear in his hand. He gestured to indicate that he was on his way back to the surface.

"Sean's all right," Nancy said to Talia. "Let's go see what Zach and the Morleys are up to on the surface."

Nancy nosed the submersible upward. As soon as they surfaced alongside the *Lady Jane,* Nancy opened the hatch and cautiously poked her head out.

"Well, well, if it isn't Nancy Drew," she heard a man announce.

Nancy turned in the direction of the voice and found herself staring down the barrel of a pistol. Zach Hardwick and Marcus Morley were aiming guns at her from the deck of the *Lady Jane.* Behind them, huddled together, were Bess and George. But where was Ned?

Nancy looked back at the armed men. Her worst fears had come true. Zach and Marcus Morley had taken the *Lady Jane* by force!

Chapter

Sixteen

GET ON BOARD, you two. Now!" Marcus Morley snapped at Nancy and Talia. He waved his gun at them from his position on the *Lady Jane*'s deck.

What's happened to Ned? Nancy kept repeating to herself. She tried to control her terror as she and Talia climbed slowly out of the sub onto the ship.

"Welcome aboard," Zach said sarcastically. He prodded Nancy with the gun's muzzle until she reached the spot where Bess and George were being held at gunpoint.

"Is Ned all right?" Nancy whispered anxiously.

"Oh, Nancy," Bess's voice squeaked with fear. "Ned tried to fight them off. Marcus knocked him out cold and took him below."

Talia's face darkened with rage as she glared at Zach. "What's gotten into you?" she asked angrily.

Zach shrugged. "I tried to warn you away from Sean, Talia," he explained, "but you wouldn't listen."

"You *didn't* tell me that you were a murdering thief!" Talia retorted.

"Calm down, Talia," Nancy whispered. "You'll only make things worse."

"Where's Sean?" George asked as if she were afraid to hear the answer. "Is he—"

"Sean's all right," Nancy said under her breath. In the distance, Nancy could see Hank Morley's sub tied up to his wooden boat. Hank was moving about on the deck of the other vessel. He's probably collecting what he needs to sink the *Lady Jane,* Nancy thought uneasily.

George now followed Nancy's glance. "The bearded guy—Marcus—threatened to shoot us unless we let him on board," George said under her breath. "He held a gun on us until Zach and Hank Morley came back to the surface."

Nancy leaned over to whisper in George's ear. "Hank Morley intends to sink the *Lady Jane*—with us on board. Do you know whether Ned was able to send the distress call?" she asked.

George shook her head. "I'm not sure," she muttered. "He was still tinkering with the radio when Marcus stormed the ship."

Nancy was thinking fast. She scanned the ocean. She wanted to spot Sean as soon as he surfaced.

Hank Morley headed toward the *Lady Jane* in the motorized dinghy. As he boarded their ship, Nancy could see that he was carrying a small wooden crate.

Opening the crate, Hank pulled out a mass of wires attached to a lump of putty.

Talia's face blanched when she saw Morley's contraption. "He's got plastic explosive," she said in a trembling voice. "They must be planning to blow us up."

Bess closed her eyes and moaned softly.

"He's not going to blow up the ship if I can help it," Nancy muttered. She leaned back to whisper to Talia. "When Sean surfaces, Hank and the others will be distracted. That may be our best chance to make a move."

Nancy noted the locations of each of their three captors. Marcus Morley and Zach were conferring several feet away from her. Hank Morley stood farther down the side of the ship, gingerly examining the explosive device in his hand.

"Tell me one thing, Zach," Talia said, glaring at him. "Did you kill my brother, Jaime?"

Zach shook his head. "No. I didn't have anything to do with that. There really must have been something wrong with his tank," he replied.

"To tell the truth, his death set the stage for this whole scheme," he continued. "People wanted to believe in a curse—so we created one."

Nancy suddenly spotted Sean's head surfacing in the water near Hank Morley. Sean was still clutching Zach's fishing spear.

Hardwick and Marcus Morley were the next to spot Sean. They turned toward him and started to fire their guns.

"Now!" Nancy yelled.

She, George, and Talia charged forward. Nancy's foot shot out with a lightning-quick karate kick that folded Zach in half.

At the same moment Talia and George sent Marcus Morley sprawling with flying tackles.

Nancy whirled around, looking for Hank. He had dropped the plastic explosive, she saw, and was reaching for his gun.

Nancy sprinted across the deck toward him. With another deft kick, she sent the gun skittering away. Bess came up behind Nancy and helped her grab his arms.

Hank twisted away from them and dove overboard. For a moment it looked as if he might make it to the other boat. Then Sean swam up behind Morley. He held him at bay with the spear, preventing his escape.

Nancy checked back to see what was happening with the other two. Talia and Bess had jumped on Zach and were pummeling him. Marcus Morley was still sprawled across the deck, knocked out cold.

Then Nancy heard a low, vibrating noise in the distance. She heaved a sigh of relief. A huge helicopter was making its way toward them across the water.

"Look, guys. It's the Coast Guard!" Nancy exclaimed. "Ned must have been able to send that SOS, after all."

"Nancy!" Her heart soared with joy at the sound of a familiar voice behind her. It was Ned! Nancy whirled about and saw him approaching from the rear, rubbing his head. Before he even reached her, she threw herself into his arms.

"Here's to you, Nancy," Sean said, raising his glass. "You saved my life *and* the treasure."

It was late afternoon the following day. Nancy, Sean, Bess, George, Talia, and Leif Dorning were celebrating in Sean's favorite restaurant, the Skipper's Loft.

Leif Dorning took a sip of his soda. "I can't believe everything that's happened," he said, reaching over to hug Talia. "I'm glad we were able to bury the hatchet," he said, smiling at Sean.

"Me, too," Ned said with a grin. "What's in store for Zach and the Morleys?"

"They're going to get a long, long vacation in prison." The satisfaction was evident in Sean's voice. "They were arraigned this morning on a bunch of charges—including Rusty's murder. Thank goodness I was cleared of it."

"And you're rich!" Bess squealed happily. "I heard a reporter saying the treasure will be worth millions when it's brought to the surface."

Sean nodded. He looked at George and smiled shyly. "Speaking of things to treasure—I have something for you, George," he said, reaching into his pocket. He pulled out a jewelry box and offered it to George.

George blushed and shook her head. "I can't accept anything expensive, Sean," she protested.

Sean smiled. "Just open it," he insisted gently.

George opened the box. Inside was a delicate seashell attached to a silver cord.

George gasped. "It's the shell we found when we were walking on the beach the other day!" she exclaimed. She leaned over and hugged Sean. "Thank you," she said.

Nancy watched the two of them. She and George had talked about Sean earlier that day, and Nancy felt good about the way her friend was handling things. George had decided to spend time with the treasure hunter during the rest of the vacation, but she knew that neither she nor Sean was in any position to make a commitment.

"Hey, Drew," Ned said, touching Nancy lightly on the shoulder. "Come outside with me. I want to show you something."

The two of them strolled through a side door onto a deck that overlooked the peaceful ocean. They stood at the railing, silent for a moment.

"So what was it you wanted me to see?" Nancy asked finally.

Ned grinned. "That was just a clever ruse to get you all to myself." He put his arm around her and drew her close. "And now that I've got you, I don't plan to let you go."

"We still have a little more time together," Nancy said. "Think of all the fun things we can do."

"My thoughts exactly," Ned replied. "And if any new mysteries turn up, they'll just have to wait, because Nancy Drew is on vacation."

Nancy laughed softly and leaned back against Ned's chest. She raised her eyes as a sea gull wheeled overhead. The bird spread its wings and glided gently downward until it vanished against the setting sun.

Nancy's next case:

Everybody's talking about "Marcy," Chicago's hip new teen TV talk show, and Nancy has tickets to see it live. When host Marcy Robbins grabs the mike and goes on the air, there's sure to be plenty of fast talk and shock-filled fireworks. But the biggest surprise of all is directed straight at Marcy: an anonymous threat on her life!

Professional rivalry . . . personal jealousy . . . crazy love . . . relationships out of control. . . . They're not the topics of Marcy's show, they're just a small sample of the secret intrigue churning and burning behind the scenes. Nancy's digging up all the dirt, searching for the single obsession powerful enough to incite a passion for murder . . . in *LET'S TALK TERROR*, Case #86 in The Nancy Drew Files™.